For the dark destroyer

First published in 2011

White Cube
25-26 Mason's Yard
London SW1Y 6BU
Tel: +44 (0) 20 7930 5373

www.whitecube.com

Murray & Sorrell FUEL ©
Design & Publishing
33 Fournier Street
London E1 6QE

www.fuel-design.com

Designed by Murray & Sorrell FUEL
Printed in China

Distributed by Thames & Hudson
ISBN: 978-0-9568962-1-6

Jake Chapman

INTROSPASTIC:
From the
Blackened Beyond

FUEL   White Cube

Let us be aware of saying that death is the opposite of life. The living being is only a species of the dead, and a very rare species.

Friedrich Nietzsche, *The Gay Science*

When I said that I was going to be a comedian they all laughed – well, they're not laughing now.

Bob Monkhouse

Chapter One

'Me? You want *me* to pretend to be a fortune teller? To divine the future and converse with the dead?' Chlamydia Love observes the old woman on the bed before her, stricken in sweat and bosom heaving. Ali Paco leans over his beloved mate with a piece of cowpoke wisdom.

'Listen crystal tips, you just take the bull by the horns. She can tell fortunes in her sleep, sleep-walking.'

Chlamydia defers to the archaic soul now reduced to degrading childish whimpers.

'Look at her! She couldn't tell past from present, let alone predict the future! What a pair! She's delirious and you're deluded! You can't possibly expect me to lie to –'

The injudicious candour is curtailed by the old woman's crabby claw, escaping the tidal pyrexia to seize her detractor's feline wrist. With sudden and uncanny lucidity an imperious tone ferments from the demented mire:

'– Yo' do it for *me* Miss Chlamydia, yo' tell de future fo' poor ol' *Maman*...'

How could Chlamydia very well resist an appeal summoned from the enervated slab of livid flesh lying prostrate on its sudor-swollen death bed? It was enough that Maman Ewe and Ali Paco had so befriended Chlamydia on the very first day she alighted at Ali Paco's World Famous Travelling Circus to undertake covert field research on a piece for *Herpes Bizarre* magazine, in her mind's eye provisionally titled, The Circus of Everyday Life. They had taken Chlamydia beneath their wing, had fussed and fed her as though she were their own flesh, blood and feather. They had even sought to protect her dignity from the lascivious attentions of the muscle men who formed the relentless pulling power of the circus. Suffice to say, Chlamydia had formed a sincere affection for her new friends, Ali Paco and Maman Ewe. They were a rare breed indeed; Ali Paco was a proud old toreros of miniature proportions and big-time responsibilities, whilst Maman Ewe was an obese Ghanaian – an irresistible force plus immovable object rolled into one adorable human boulder. Ali Paco was Boss-man of the big top and ambassador of the circus. It was his job to quell the tendentious attitudes of provincial town councils before they conspired to prevent guy ropes and tent pegs taking root in commoners' ground. But once the circus had accomplished secure erection, Maman Ewe shed the cheery-pops fat mama garb to delve deep into egregious *Maman Poisson* – an inviolate syncretic fortune teller on quick-dial to the devil. Thus, on performance night Maman Poisson powdered her matt black face eggshell white, modelled a long loose noir kaftan, fringed in sanguinary crimson, with a cinnabar silk headband in the grey black mane from which sea shells, teeth, bird feathers and dubious bone fragments dangled on braided human hair.

'Can't you give her something? Medication? Chicken soup? Magic potion?'

Ali Paco has turned taciturn, the black wisp of static hair lining his bald head shimmering in mid-air.

Maman groans at the simplicity of Chlamydia's suggestion – Chlamydia has compassion for Maman's plight, but she is too shy, too reserved to effect the deception. She'd make an absolute fool of herself and be rewarded with mockery and humiliation. So she tends to the tendrils of loose hair tickling her frowning mantle, pushing the errant curls back into the messy chignon above her luminous nape. Ali Paco's petroglyphic head is looming dangerously over his moribund otherhalf with morose presentiments of the world of grieving to follow. Wistfully adorned by vulture's quill and poised before a glowing crystal orb, Chlamydia imagines herself tongue-tied; she'd blush, and the lie emblazoned on her skin will surely betray her – an akratic chameleon found shamed by dishonest mimesis. She will surely make a fool of herself, worse still, to denude the dark arts of their mystical enchantment warrants risk of a less occultist and more pragmatic punishment – that of being lynched by the neck, chignon or not, and there are ropes everywhere in the circus – lassos, bridles, straps, leashes, ties and tethers looping like vines in a hostile jungle, opportunities for murder all around... *the night is already full of homicidal impulses*...

'Can't Maman just take the night off?' she says. 'Just put up a little note? No fortune telling tonight due to unforeseen circumstances?'

From the death bed, a mass grave of moans –

'*DE SHOW MUST GO ON...*'

Ali Paco pipes up.

'Listen Chlamydia, it don't take much to work the magic of the crystal ball, an' it don't even matter if you just... *make it all up*... Just for one night – for the sake of my poor Maman. She's never let destiny down, *not once...*'

Against better judgment, Chlamydia is secretly installed in Maman Poisson's tented booth with crystal ball set before her. As per instruction, she fumbles beneath the table to fire up the magic orb. The energy efficient light bulb groans to full luminosity, a dull, dread-filled presentiment of the dead sun and the creeping, cold, hostile, cosmic darkness to come. Nailed to a post outside, Maman Poisson's plywood sign happily declares magical wares with eschatological messages in fancy vinyl lettering:

WHY WAIT FOR THE FUTURE? FIND OUT RIGHT THIS VERY MINUTE! VISIT CLAIRVOYANT MAMAN POISSON AND HAVE YOUR ASTROLOGICAL PATH CHARTED! RUNES READ AND LOTTERY NUMBERS DIVULGED! SPEAK TO THE UNDEAD – NO BULLSHIT! TAROT! CRYSTAL BALL! PALM READING! BEHOLD TRUE LOVE'S FORM BEFORE THE SQUALOR OF UNHAPPY UNION WRECKS YOUR CHANCE FOR LONG-TERM SERENITY! GOOD NEWS! INFERTILITY SPURNED – BABIES SPAWNED! ALL FORMS OF INSIDIOUS CANCERS AND BLACK MASS SHEWN TO THE NAKED EYE! MAKE PEACE WITH THE VOICES IN YOUR HEAD BEFORE IT'S TOO LATE! AVOID THE MAGGOTS – REINCARNATION DEALS BROKERED TO PERSONAL SATISFACTION! ONLY TEN POUNDS PER SITTING! TIME WASTERS BEWARE – FOR YE SHALL REAP THE CURSE OF MAMAN POISSON AND SUFFER UNIMAGINABLE EXCRUTIATION WITH EVERY FOOTSTEP HENCEFORTH!
(senior citizen discount available on demand, no refunds, additional voices and spectral visitors free of charge)

She feels idiotic in the oversize low-cut red gown awash with scaly sequins on the bodice revealing a cleavage which had never before seen the light of day. The clingy fabric alters her anatomy too and she glitters with diamonds, all of them paste, a thin guillotine-red choker encircles her bare-necked throat and a half a dozen pewter bracelets manacle left arm from elbow to wrist plus anchor handy-pandy to hip. Maman has kindly donated earrings and rings such that Chlamydia can barely curl her fist into a tantrum, if she felt the urge. A paste diamond circlet is fixed upon tumultuous forehead and a requisite vulture's quill is poised before the glowing orb. Maman's dresser tried painting Chlamydia's verdant blush black before powdering it white, to summon Maman Poisson's sinister countenance, but all were in agreement that she had the appearance of a menstruating black and white minstrel. Instead, Chlamydia's voluptuous dictyostelidic lips are stained a cruel vermilion, eyes lined with deepwater horizon kohl, lashes thick with crude oil mascara. Instinct nevertheless urges flight, but saturated in the excess folds of Maman Poisson's ill-fitting garb, flight is doomed to a lone sack race with humiliation waiting at the finish line. So she sits and waits for the tent curtains to rudely part and the first customer to be born into her incapable clutches.

After a healthy glut of ingenuous punters have crossed Maman Poisson's palm with legal denomination, each enduring a perfunctory reading and parting company without demand for the return of their disbursement, Chlamydia gains confidence and comes swiftly to this summation: it is in the weighing up of a person's shit that the jewels of their desired destiny can be imagined. Thus, the secret of successful fortune telling is in acting upon the most shameless conjecture and barefaced prejudice – the more bigoted or blunt the better – and this simply for the fact that an unfettered presumption about a person's taste, social class or conviction of faith gives rise to counterfactual caricatures which the fortune teller thus magically projects upon the silver screen of a hankered destiny. This is how it works in the flesh: a bulging woman whose anxiety is ironed smooth by Botox, longs for her imminent newborn to be quiet, demure and sleep through the night without the blot of cot death ruining her own precious beauty sleep. Chlamydia's crystal ball sets about the task and obliges. Mummy exits the fortune teller's tent, quelled by the promise of a serene – if not quietus future. A rough-shod farmer with calluses on shovel-sized palms sows the seeds of ludicrous aspiration and no-sooner harvests a sun-blessed apparition of a sublime crop, an agreeable wife, healthy offspring and a shiny new tractor. He makes his exit purring like a cattle prod. A dishevelled young widow seeks psychic news of a more robust husband. To give the poor beleaguered woman a moment's peace, her vile progeny are coaxed to a dim corner of the tent to play 'snap' with the fortune teller's own tarot cards. Chlamydia would surely love to play snap with their little bones, but thinks better of it, mindful of the real limitations of her animistic charms upon the mortal bodies of those under her temporary spell.

A lull in business offers Chlamydia chance to reflect upon her circumstances and plan how to incorporate first-hand experiences of palm reading into her carnival critique. Just then an immature voice penetrates the stoic gloom from the outside.

'Go on. I dare you. Have your fortune told!'

'No.'

'Why not? Are you scared?'

'Scared? Me?'

'Go on *Uncle Buncle*! Don't be a chicken!'

'Okay then – *you first*!'

Thus the jeering boy is thrust forward and comes tumbling inside the tent. Once adjusted upright, he insists Chlamydia not only read his palm but divulge in molecular detail his entire future. Chlamydia obliges because the boy with freckled nose, wire-brush hair and grimy face is so pleasingly porous. He waffles without reserve and spills without prompting.

Sneaky Chlamydia is surreptitious enough to glean what the lad wishes to be when he grows up, and later on in the reading Maman Poisson hazards prediction of what the child will eventually become once mature – and amazingly, the two things are one and the same thing. Hats off to proving counterfactuals right. He talks and natters and rants and raves, but later, in his absence, Chlamydia has cause to rack her own addled spongiform to recall stories of double maths, of head teachers and arson... *And Uncle Buncle*. She hears the boy squawk about how dear old Uncle Buncle *is an artist*. She now wishes she had insisted the brat be more specific and curses her indifference to the child's incessant chatter...

'So you're the notorious Maman Poisson.'

'Very perceptive... Are you de psychic too? Two psychics in de same tent? Now what is de probability of dat? Eh?'

'Probability? Not exactly the psychic currency I expected of a *fortune teller*...'

Uncle Buncle is sad-eyed, bald, mid-forties, and, although tall, stoops inelegantly. Pallid grey skin betrays an unhygienic timidity to the sun, impassive gimlet eyes are deep-set beneath a forensic frown, but the real money is on the nose – of such comic proportions that Chlamydia is first sent cross-eyed before deeming to banish the obscene protuberance from fixation before falling prey to churlish giggles. Enervating light from the crystal ball ambles over her sitter, having the odd affect of making him appear waxen – or *molten*.

'How may Maman Poisson be of service to your fate?'

'Tell me what the future holds...' He flattens a worn ten pound note on the table, the Queen's tired old worn-out haggard filthy dirty gaze is sullied by the exchange of endless filthy dirty hands handling her. Chlamydia's own crabby claw grabs the besmirched tender and sticks it in a pot. In a vague courtship of ellipses, she casts both hands about the tepid orb as though warming her palms above a winter radiator.

'Let me consult de crystal ball... oh... oh yes! Oh yes, yes, yes... oh... I see it with my eyes... yes... I see... see... de creation! *Much* creation in your past! *Much* creation in your present!' Maman Poisson defers to a pregnant pause – schism of the undead reaching up from hell, voice deepening, eyes tilting upwards like the brief doomed flare of exploding suns that registers dimly on blind men's eyes, the surfeit gasp of solar decay...

'Wait... wait... wait... it's... going... no... no... going... no... going... going... going... going... going...'

'Don't let it go! DON'T LET IT GO! WHAT IS IT SAYING? *DON'T GO PLEASE!*'

'Going... going... *gone.*' And with that, Chlamydia's eyes roll and settle back down into the seat of mortal realm. She awakes from her uncanny dimensional intrusion to find Uncle Buncle sprung like an anti-personnel mine, his knuckles are all apoplectic white. His mean little eyes have dispensed of the need to blink, presumably wishing not to miss anything, and instead he nods at Chlamydia, silently urging her to speak. But all is doomed.

'I sorry... it gone now. I say no more... it gone *forever*... I so sorry...'

Uncle Buncle explodes to his feet with obdurate rage.

'I UNDERSTOOD THE BIT ABOUT MY PAST AND MY PRESENT – YES! – BUT WHAT ABOUT THE FUTURE? WHAT ABOUT THE FUTURE OF MY CREATIVITY, EH? YOU MUST TELL ME BECAUSE I NEED TO KNOW! DO YOU UNDERSTAND? I HAVE TO KNOW! IT'S A NEED TO KNOW BASIS – AND I NEED TO KNOW! ESPECIALLY NOW!'

'Yo' must be patient with de crystal ball... De crystal ball hurries for no man...'

Uncle Buncle crumples to his chair, stricken down and seated.

'Please tell me... please...'

'Your palm... give me.'

Chlamydia takes his in hers and draws a fathomless breath. Tapping down into the unseeable reservoir of unresolved tragedies poisoning the fossil fuel of her own emotional life. Thus she summons up the blackest thoughts, taps the most destructive subductive powers, the most crude and audacious traumas contorting her soul. Real-life tears freely purge from unobstructed ducts, now weeping inconsolably like a child over a dead kitten, but there's more than one way to skin a cat, and heaving with such disarticulated grief, poor Uncle Buncle can do nothing but snatch his tainted palm from the disconsolate fortune teller...

'What is it? What can you see? *You must tell me! YOU MUST!'*

'It's nothing... I see nothing... saw nothing... Forget you ever came here and set eyes upon Maman Poisson or her crystal ball! I beg of you!' Chlamydia shields her eye s. 'BE GONE!... MY EYES... MY EYES... MY EYES! AAAAAAEEEEEEEEEEEEEEEEEEEEEEEEEOOOOOO O? √ ? Âô !˜, †zô ?!˜†zô !˜. †zô !˜/ †zô !˜0 †zô ?!˜1 †zô3 †zô !˜4 †zô ?!˜5 †zô !˜ ??=!??"?T9h9i9s b9e9i9n9g is a man whose m9a9n9-9h9o9l9e9s are v9i9b9r9a9t9i9n9g i9n9c u 9 n 9 t 9 e 9 n 9 t

._____

_____¢›fi››‡flfiflfifl_____a e_____ H y p o g l y c a e m i a?0 ??? p9e9e9l9i9n9g9i9n9s9i9d9e9-o9u9t?? ?she?? ? ??tells me not to panic ? ?$?a$? ? 1 (r)f @ 1 (tm)f @ 1 ?? 1 s9e9r9v9i9l9i9t9y to who? To her, she's practically *the fucking ringleader* – 10n10o10t 10t10o10 p10a10n10i10c 10?'

With fear stapled to petrified countenance, Uncle Buncle clambers to his feet, staggers backwards into his chair, unable to tear himself from Maman's necromantic tongue, and emitting his own outrageous castrati yelp, the towering buffoon turns to escape into the circus and the candy floss night. Chlamydia is thus overcome by an exultant sense of having just struck oil. She could pack writing in and make a fortune telling fortunes full-time. She cackles out loud but the crystal ball flickers, flares and fuses – the tent falls silent.

Chapter Two

'Dear Chlamydia, I can't tell you how relieved I am to be able to tell you in person what a devious bitch you are! *Come here!*' Chlamydia shrinks inside her brother's bear hug as he hoists her, mindful of the gap, from train to platform at award-winning Royal Tunbridge Wells, repatriation set down for middle England's dreary departed.

'What do you mean?' she says, taken aback by his booby-trap welcome.

'*You don't write, you don't phone* – we've taken to following articles in bloody newspapers and magazines to see how you're getting on! The *Herpes Bizarre* piece was a bloody joy! Posing as a fortune teller to mess with the destiny of the poor unwitting *Untermensch*? You should be bloody ashamed of yourself!'

'Oh that! It's out already?'

'I just loved poor old Uncle Buncle fleeing the tent with his stupid big nose! What an utterly divine twat!'

'Did they butcher it?'

'Well that's an odd thing to say.'

'Well they always do.'

'Well you mustn't let them.'

'I don't exactly have the choice.'

'We all have choices, Chlamydia... Remember, life is the sum of all your choices.'

'– Or it's an almighty disappointment crowned by a minor tragedy.'

'But the suicide bomber straps a bomb to himself in the Name of God, whilst the astronaut straps himself to a rocket in the Name of the Cosmos.'

'To hell with God and Cosmos, my rule of thumb is this –

things that can go wrong, *will*.'

The good-natured banter continues all the way to Lomax's house, a tidy country cottage perched atop a quaint tuffet enjoying glorious views of Kent's barbed-wire lattice and the sad biomass captured within its bounds. It is the kind of urbane bickering brother and sister cherish on account of being twins – all other similarities terminating just after birth. Hence, it would be a statement of pure banality to mention that Chlamydia is easier on the eye than Lomax Love, simply because Lomax is baffled by unfair gravity, is unfairly rotund plus suffers full blown psoriasis and a raging constellation of angry freckles wreaking havoc to the civility of his countenance. As if to inure the world from his displeasing appearance, Lomax's personality is a breath of purest fresh air.

Two long months have elapsed since Chlamydia posted her written observations on the carnival of everyday life and she is feeling particularly enervated. Under the circumstances of mental exhaustion and finding herself voluntarily chaste, she happily accepted Lomax's merciful invitation to deliver herself into his benevolent charity for a few days, to amble in the valley with the dogs, to hunt for antiques in the charming Georgian Pantiles colonnade and to warm her aching cold heart on the hearty sustenance heated up on the burning hot Aga.

'Jesus wept! You look like a death-camp warmed-up!' Thus Sandy Love's pithy gambit greets Chlamydia from the bare-boned passenger seat of Lomax's sturdy all-terrain Defender.

'Are you ill, sleep-deprived? On drugs? If so, which drugs are responsible for making you ill and which drugs are depriving you of sleep?'

Chlamydia is fond of her sister-in-law, not least because she is the perfect foil for her ebullient brother, but also because she is a rare and complex specimen, tormented by an ill-fitting identity which she absolutely insists upon – the prim, pragmatic and trenchantly sensible caricature whom Lomax first engaged as a dependable PA before engaging his faithful PA to be his loyal wife. Chlamydia has an affection for tortured souls. She finds being mad amongst lunatics allows her own episodic disturbances to appear more mundane. Lomax Love is big in advertising, and his celebrated brainchild, NO HOLDS BARRED ADVERTISING AGENCY, is epitomised by blockbusting campaigns like the Australian Tourist Board's WHO SAID CRIME DOESN'T PAY? or the United Arab Emirates Tourist Board's BETTER LEGLESS IN DUBAI THAN LIMBLESS IN SAUDI ARABI or the Japanese Tourist Board's EVERY MUSHROOM CLOUD HAS A SILVER LINING. Executive Lomax no longer employs himself to come up with snappy catchphrases, but he can't quite switch off the marketing monster cogitating like an evil steam-driven hard-drive inside, so it is Sandy's job to bring Lomax crashing back down to earth, and she does so with leaden aplomb. For instance:

'Dear, dear Chlamydia! Oh dear! I read you like a pop-up book. The very moment I laid eyes on you I could tell you've been surviving on junk, partying on your back and selling yourself too cheap! The first thing I'm going to do is sit you down and give you a slap-up meal because you look like an anorexic Eastern European with a gut stuffed full of smack-filled condoms being teased by a customs official in no particular hurry and with a hard-on for sex slaves. Have you being doing drugs? *Which ones…*'

'Don't be a bore, darling,' says hubby. 'Remember: there are only two emotions in a plane, boredom and terror.'

'Is that so? Well British Airways didn't buy it and nor am I – so don't try fobbing off your reject jingles on me, Sweetie Pants!'

Lomax blushes beyond the saturation of an already violent hue.

'You two lovebirds! *Really!*' protests Chlamydia, with mixed affection.

The Loves' guest room is decorated in lime-green and lemon-yellow. The whimsical colour scheme betrays rare dispensation to Lomax's own sensibility on account of the fact that during more turbulent times within the Love household he often finds himself a guest in his own house, and thus settles his steaming head upon septic-green and cholera-yellow pillows. Chlamydia casts her Samsonite upon the floor, attention stolen by the copy of *Herpes Bizarre* purposefully placed upon the guest bed, spread-eagled in full glory. Chlamydia kicks off her slingbacks and snuggles up, beady eyes scanning the text for editorial damage.

THE CIRCUS OF EVERYDAY LIFE
by Chlamydia Love

'Me? You want *me* to stand-in as Maman Ewe – the world-famous circus fortune teller?' Blood drains from my face at the dizzying prospect. The wiry old gaucho they call Ali Paco leans over his sickly mate to impart a piece of circus wisdom just for my benefit.

'Listen crystal tips, you just gotta take the bull by its horns. Maman can tell fortunes even in her sleep!' I observe the poor soul laid out on her sick bed, stricken in sweat, bosom heaving. It occurs to me right then and there that the poor soul couldn't tell past from present let alone predict the future. What a pair! She's delirious and he's deluded! But before I can protest my case Maman's hand seizes upon my wrist and with sudden and uncanny lucidity she says –

'Yo' do it for me Miss Chlamydia, yo' tell de future fo' poor Maman Ewe...' How could I very well resist such a demand? Maman Ewe and Ali Paco had been so wonderfully accommodating from the very first second I arrived at their circus to mix with their circus brethren – the bedlam of acrobats, jugglers, mimes, horses and clowns. The couple had taken such an incandescent shine to me, incubated me beneath their wing, they had fussed and fed me as though I were their own flesh and blood. They had even protected me from the attentions of the red-blooded muscle men who formed the relentless pulling power of the circus. Not that I minded the attention, you understand...

Ali Paco is a diminutive man with enormous responsibilities. He is boss of the big top and patriarch to all who reside beneath the sanctuary of its grand old tarpaulin. Looming over Ali Paco is Maman Ewe, an irresistible force and immovable object all rolled into one loveable bundle. Each evening Maman Ewe makes her magical transformation into the elegiac figure of High Priestess Maman Poisson, and had she not been so poorly, she would be adorned in a carbon black Bahraini kaftan fringed in crimson, a rare Syrian cinnabar silk band in her grey black mane from which sea shells dangle eerily on braided Egyptian silk.

'Isn't there anything you can give her? Pills? Medication?' I'm admittedly clutching at straws. Ali Paco shakes his head and looks upon his other half with the saddest Spanish eyes this side of Gibraltar. Imagination suddenly invents a peculiar trick. I see myself adorned in Maman's garb, poised before the glowing crystal orb. An expectant man sits before me, but I am tongue-tied, blushing like a gawky schoolgirl at morning worship. My skin betrays the pretence, and frustrated by shattered dreams, my bemoaning client sees fit to demand his good money back – worse still, Maman's good name is now unfairly dragged through the mud and both she and Ali Paco are cruelly exiled from the circus in a mocking ancient ritual involving glue, being heckled and sprinkled with horse hair and urine...

'Couldn't Maman just take the night off?' I say.

From the deathbed a six-foot-deep groan –

'Chlamydia, my dearest friend, de show must go on...'

In the newly fitted country-look kitchen, with its rustic simplicity and practical honesty, its mixed fabrics in shades of weathered slate and stone, Chlamydia discovers Sandy slicing tomatoes.

'There you are! Can I help?'

Sandy turns with a cherry ripe smile and a cheeky plum wink.

'If you like you could help chopping, y'know, *chop, chop, chop...*'

Companionably side by side, they sip an arid Rhodesian Chablis and chew the fat about inconsequential things whilst slicing 'n' dicing organic bits 'n' pieces for a delish fresh 'n' wild salad. Sandy explains how she still insists on three days at Lomax's agency whilst devoting the rest of her time to the potter's wheel. One of the rooms in the house is thus set aside for Sandy's messy hobby. Chlamydia customarily suggests Sandy market her craft products in London, Paris, New York and possibly even Beijing. Sandy sighs as she passes wobbly hand-made plates for lunch down from the stripped pine top shelf.

'I just don't have the energy these days...'

'How so? But they're so very beautiful – the colours and iridescent glazes are so luminous, so vivid, so vivacious, *so you!* You know how I adore the matt beige ash tray you created for my thirtieth.'

'Well, if truth be told,' lures Sandy, 'I'm not going to have too much time for sticky old mud and pooey old clay in the weeks and months to come.'

'You don't mean... ?'

'Yes I do. I *do* mean...'

'You mean...'

'Yes! Yes! I *mean*...' Sandy lassos Chlamydia in a smothering embrace. 'Can you believe it? I'm going to make you an aunt! Aunty Chlamydia! How d'you like that? Eh? Aunty Chlamydia? Old spinster aunty Chlamydia!'

'But I thought... Didn't the doctors say you were...'

'Barren? Dry? Parched as a Dead Sea Scroll? Well, let me tell you, after notching up more midnight miscarriages than you've had morning-after pills, *the specialists* declared I was too hysterical to conceive – as far as all *the specialists* were concerned my poor little sausage-snatcher was kaput! No womb in the inn for me! Well bollocks to them – it's from here to maternity for us!'

'Sandy *please!*' Lomax casts an awkward glance at his sister, the raging freckles on his face speaking volumes. Foil to Lomax's ebullient-less freckles, Sandy comes to sharpish –

'I'm so, so, so sorry Chlamydia,' says Sandy clutching Chlamydia's unfortunate palm. 'I really wasn't thinking... Can you ever forgive me Aunty Chlamydia?' Her grip tightening and teeth gritted. 'Ever?'

'Oh don't be silly!' says Aunty Chlamydia. 'It's wonderful news, and anyway I've put all that silly old stuff far behind me... I'm fine with it. I really am!'

After an indigestible lunch and a sickly-sweet desert that stuck in the craw before summarily offending the taste buds with bilious refrain, Chlamydia makes excuses to accompany the Loves' adorable twin labs, Genghis and Khan, to maraud deep into the valley – pursuing the meandering banks of the vast reservoir, past the pumping station and skimming close to the raw concrete sewerage plant secluded in the silver birch wood. There, the sound of berating woodpeckers cross-fades with the internal trepanning deep in Chlamydia's own mind. So she perches for a moment on a natural outcrop, worn to dirt by lone fishermen angling for the make-do intimacy of cold-eyed tench or evil-eyed pike. Gathering thoughts and a flat stone to lazily cast into the water. It skips over the surface with three magical bounces before being swallowed with a gutless plop. She tries again but only scores two skips, then one skip and then none. With resolute effort she casts another stone but receives not even a single skip for the trouble, and as the lifeless projectile sinks into the rotten sludge marring the dyspnoeic reservoir bed, a familiar portal opens in Chlamydia's own murky depths. An unnameable event in an unmentionable past now demands yet another audience with her shell-like. But how these cheeks dimple so sweetly, whilst inside she buckles so deeply! How melancholia harbours vanity in the heart! Enraptured by the opportunity for sorrow, Chlamydia risks self-pity at grievous cost – this is an itch she has scratched to the bone and a bone she has gnawed to the bare knuckle! *It's wonderful news, and anyway I've put all that silly old stuff far behind me... I'm fine with it. I really am...* The next missile lifted by fair hand is an obdurate rock – clumsy and malformed – with pitted surface yet to be smoothed by Nature's intemperate erosion. Chlamydia hurls the mass with all her might, intent on creating a garish splash smack-bang in the ground zero of the Kentian sublime. There, before her mind's eye, the ripples of the rock's sudden immersion are magnified a billion times until an infinitely exaggerated wall of filthy water churns up Kent and the whole countryside resembles a burst sewer bobbing with tides of excrement –

even the reservoir vomits its own freshwater species to bloat and explode on high ground under the murderous scrutiny of the sun. Once again Chlamydia sees how the populations of water and land are destined to a merciless exchange. She sees how the evil world is set against itself – earth, wind, fire and water – water against land, land against water – a pernicious marriage formed of elemental jeopardy. Chlamydia smiles. Only Nature's tendential violence gives rise to that opportune cheerfulness permitted by the noble precipitations of human struggle – *charity born of tragedy*. A mild shiver wriggles down Chlamydia's back as the oversized worm of human piety gorges on her spinal cord. She summons up thought of the burgeoning stupidity of her present disposition, struggles to shake off the nagging confession that her own happiness is a willing friend to wretchedness. To curb the tugging threads of an archaic masochism, Chlamydia recalls the clutch of ornamental secretions contributing a temporary respite from the involuntary momentum of her life – to home comforts like her flat, her Smart car and cuddly pussycat 'Ms Lollypop' – but, most of all, she thinks of her writing *and like clock-work, cheerfulness slips like silt through fingers. She buckles in the imagination of destiny eagerly creeping to meet her in the form of maggots and the primitive guts of worms – she gasps out loud in the realisation that time is little more than a sanitised abstraction of creeping ruination – she groans out loud in the realisation that her mind is as always being stalked by the relentless nibble of the maggot jaws ticking away in the shadows of the grasping hands of the human clock... tick... tock, that life is one long and drawn-out death...*

Sometime later Sandy discovers Aunty Chlamydia shivering next to the reservoir. Petulant clouds have swept in from the east, accompanied by a spiteful autumn breeze whipping Chlamydia's loose hair around her turbulent head. Sandy carefully drapes a cashmere blanket around her sister-in-law's shoulders, drawing the shawl to a close about the front of her frail frame.

'Penny for your thoughts?'

Deep inside Aunty Chlamydia's infernal core, nightmarish apparitions are threatening to cross the brittle threshold of her sanity, mental ogres casting bleak abstract silhouettes onto the dank cave wall behind. She cowers in the knotted belly of her own memory, willing the unwelcome procession to pass, but as the nefarious silhouettes lope by, the grotesquely fearful figurine bringing up the rear – Grumpy, or Sleepy or maybe Dopey – unexpectedly rounds on Chlamydia. Outstretched before a poached ivory leer, a human foetus dangles, bloodied and prematurely mired, the poor wretch untimely ripp'd...

'Penny for my thoughts?' You couldn't cunting-well afford it...

•   •   •   •   •

The question of commitment was uppermost in Chlamydia's mind when she thumbed a brief SMS to Trent Weir to join her for supper at St John's Bread and Wine in London's esoteric East End. Chlamydia has procrastinated long enough by allowing her writing assignments to postpone the little *tête-à-tête* she now intends to have with her man-friend. The choice of restaurant is tailor-made to suit Trent on account of Trent being an avid vegetarian, and Chlamydia sincerely doubts whether he will stomach the no-nonsense nose-to-tail menu. Agonised flesh will sour Trent's appetite before his tongue is tied when Chlamydia reveals her intention to sever relations and call it quits.

'I'm so thrilled you managed to steal yourself away from your workload to see me because I know how busy you are and I'm really so flattered you took time out to meet me and to sit down and eat, even though I'm sure you're up against it and probably would have eaten in your writing office, a tomato and basil brioche or fresh sashimi or a simple pastry or whatnot – what with all your deadlines and all. It's such a treat to see you – and you do look so very radiant, so utterly beautiful – it's quite astonishing how you manage it – with your burgeoning workload, I mean.'

Trent steals Chlamydia's absent hand from the stem of her wine glass. She allows her hand to suffer his petting, observing the spasmic prattle through a foul thicket of tarantula lashes. Any sane person would consider her to be making a grave mistake. After all, Trent is a Royal Institute of British Architects architect. He designed and built his own dream house. He possesses a kind heart, an expensive car, underground parking and an avid interest in all things highbrow. After just a few weeks being customarily charmed by Trent's tireless affection, Chlamydia could boast slumbering through more operas and sleepwalking through more retrospectives than you've had gourmet dinners. He had whisked her away to Paris, Marrakech and the Black Forest – garnished her with elegant couture, exotic Moorish amulets and even bestowed an antique Jagdstück Buddhist cuckoo clock purloined from the Deutsches Uhrenmuseum. Yet Trent's whistle-stop tour had neglected to pay lip service to one excitable region – Chlamydia's *heart*, and hence, the poor man is now paying for the disappointment – now bound by an unwitting obligation to observe a strange carnivorous smile forming on Chlamydia's face, as the abattoir of malicious intent grinds into action.

'Shall we order? I can't quite decide between the *grilled ox heart & celeriac* or the *roast bone marrow & parsley salad*. Then again, the *calf's liver & swede* looks very tempting. Anything grab your fancy?'

Rarely is salad an emphatic choice, more frequently an act of reluctant observance. Not today.

'Salad.'

'The lambs' tongues are especially tender here. They store the lambs out the back in a pretty little pen. All nice and fresh. If you listen you can hear them bleat! Listen! The chef once told me, *the better they bleat, the nicer to eat... BA-A-A-AAAA!'*

'Chlamydia, why do you persist in teasing me so?'

'What about yummy venison offal? Or chitterlings? How about woodcock? You'd like woodcock... *all hard and fowl.'*

She detaches her hand from his. She didn't have to be told she was beautiful. Her white silk suit flattered her slender figure; the navy and red blouse brought out the vivid tones of her delicate colouring; and the murder of crow black hair had been styled high on her sculptural head. She turns heads wherever she goes, and could not care less for the wake of interest in the surface of things. Damn appearances! Damn her contagious good looks and blackest black hair. Is it all they ever think about? *ARE THEY OBSESSED?* Chlamydia shifts uneasily in her chair as the waiter cranes, keen to take orders and press on.

'May I have the lamb's tongue, rare, with seasonal greens please?'

'And for sir –'

'SALAD!'

The waiter licks his lips and limps to the kitchen with a Sheffield glint in his good eye.

'Did you have a nice time with your wonderful brother Lomax and his lovely wife Sandy and their two lovely dogs Khan and Genghis? I'd love to come with you and meet them the next time you visit them. I know you went alone this time because you were exhausted from all that writing, writing,

writing. I hope it was restful for you and you feel better for it –'

Chlamydia fingers her soured wine glass, wondering if and when this loquacious purge will end. Perhaps Trent's adoration might place enough stress upon his cardiovascular system, send him into arrest and kill him outright. Chlamydia Love finds herself curiously mindful of the last woman to be executed in Britain in 1955 – the aptly named Ruth Ellis.

'How much do you love me?'

'So much – I can't tell you!'

'TRY...' Ruthless.

Trent's face suffers a sudden ignominious prolapse, expression drained in gravity's claw. Chlamydia goes in for the kill.

'I've been thinking, Trent. We've been seeing too much of one another.'

'What do you mean? We hardly ever see each other. You're always working.'

'We're both too fond of our independence to get involved at this point in our careers.'

'I'm not. I don't want to be all *independent*. I want to be all cosy and snug-as-a-bug with you in our little love nest, just you and me against the world!'

Chlamydia's heart sinks in comprehension of the uphill task in hand. Her hands are twisting at the starched napkin in her lap and forming an imaginary garrotte.

'I thought you *liked* me.' Trent's falsetto now shrill enough to pierce the ears of other patrons.

'I've had a wonderful time with you, dearest Trent... I'll never forget our times together, the ups, the downs – the handcuffs and helium, the jelly and cream... naughty but nice!'

Trent ignores the bowl of extra creamy vichyssoise being

placed on the table before him to impart a hint of the bitterness to follow.

'Who wouldn't enjoy orchestra seats to the ballet and theatre, the sojourns to Calais, the sight-seeing and all the exotic jewellery, the VIP perks and the endless corporate freebies?'

'Oh Trent! Don't be so bloody vulgar! You know that's not the reason...'

'Do I Chlamydia?'

'I'm not saying we're incompatible, it's just that compatibility doesn't always lead to true love – and I so-o-o-o prefer to be head-over-heels!'

'Heels? *Cobblers!* You've managed long enough with me. You think I haven't noticed how you keep me at arm's length – I mean, how could I not notice being kept at arm's length? You think it doesn't hurt that you're habitually tepid – customarily lukewarm – that even friction fails to ignite intimacy? I prayed you'd warm up. More fool me! It's crystal clear now, because what I see before me is the tip of a frigid iceberg and I'm HMS bloody TITANIC – steaming full-steam ahead without a care in the world and cast-iron love... *on bloody collision course with the destroyer of dreams!*'

The woman on the next table casts a withering glance at HMS Titanic sinking into the frozen depths.

'Please, Trent, there's no need to be like that...'

'No... I'm sorry... I apologise. It's a lady's prerogative, and all that... I'm just awfully upset. I suppose brave Captain Weir must go down with his ship!'

To add insult to injury, Chlamydia's lamb's tongue arrives, swimming adrift in the ensanguinated *jus* of its own mutilation.

'Mmmm yummy!' says Chlamydia, licking her sticky gloss lips.

Like two stricken boat buoys, Trent's eyeballs bulge beyond

the tensile tolerance of their anatomical mooring. Even his bilge announces its discontent, sluicing his mouth with bile upon taste bud.

'Good God! That's it! I can't take any more! How on earth did I manage to fall for a woman who devours lambs' tongues, *rare, with seasonal bloody greens?*' The gentle shepherd rises to his feet and with a single disgorging belch poorly muffled by hand, turns for the door. 'Insensate bitch!'

And with that, Trent Weir is no more.

● ● ● ● ●

Chlamydia's flat proves to be little sanctuary from disturbing thoughts. The indefatigable cast of sentient extras routinely populating her torrid nightmares are always quick to hand, seeking consort with self-doubt at the drop of Goneril's very own hat – keen to tread the creaking boards of Chlamydia's inner psychodrama. Locking and bolting the heavy duplex doors to keep the outside world out does little more than secure the injurious tragedians backstage, given paradoxical sanctuary inside her very own psychosis – still, Trent is now a thing of the past – and that's a good thing. Thus calmed, moon-minded distraction prowls the flat, sees fit to absentmindedly straighten up the *frete* cushions on the recliner, fluffing and fretting, punching them in – just like she straightened out Trent. Likewise the sheet music on the spinet piano is roughly rearranged with an atonal discordant Trent in mind, before the cherished bookshelf is found – itself a shrine to Chlamydia's self-blossoming. There, a finger caresses the book spines, one-by-one, teasing each distinctive title, embossed or not – 'HOW TO PUT HUMPTY DUMPTY BACK TOGETHER AGAIN', 'NEW TRICKS FOR OLD DOGS', 'SAY BYE-BYE TO BIPOLAR DISORDER', 'RE-BIRTHING FOR DUMMIES', 'GET OVER IT! A

HURDLER'S TALE ABOUT LOW SELF-ESTEEM', 'A
BLUFFER'S GUIDE TO TREPANNING', 'HOW TO
HELP YOURSELF TO SELF HELP IN SEVEN
HELPFUL STEPS'. As though the compulsion to this very
place were ever in doubt, the finger arrests its loving motion,
manoeuvred to an old, implacable friend – 'DEPRESSION:
HOW TO TAKE IT FROM BEHIND', by Chlamydia's ex-
therapist and psychic mentor, Doctor Heimlich. With the
elect opus in hand, Chlamydia reclines, the supernatural
tension in the spine turns a page or two before a bygone
weakness in its binding lays open a well-thumbed passage. The
reader is so moved to read aloud, comforted by an indefatigable
conviction that, despite its exculpatory anonymity, the clinical
origin of this exquisite passage derives from observations the
eminent Doctor Heimlich once made about her most cherished
of patients – *her patient's patient* – Chlamydia Love, all those
many full moons ago:

When one wakes up to the mechanics of one's own autonomic
monotony, when one can no longer remain unconsciously
persuaded that this is *enough*... it's time for the impostor inside
of us to be thrown to her knees before us, and serious questions
asked: What do you want of me? What is this vast and
universal mockery called 'life'? What is this horizon of infinite
horrors which you compel me to towards on your behalf? Why
am I forced to follow these ineluctable forces, when day
perishes and night suffocates ME, ME, ME, and I am called
to venture into the psychic underworld? What if I fail to find
an anchor for my own vertigo? – thus to cascade towards
obliteration, social sodomy or abstinence from the paternal
ascendancy of mammalian reproduction? Can a simplistic
hankering for stochastic certainty calm the inchoate waters of
the fluid world around me? Must you drown and drag me with

you? What specific purpose is there to sentience? – once self preservation is shown to be a sham, to Know that God is a farce and that we must all die lonely? What is it for the tongue to turn to stone, the cell to scale, for warm hearts to cool and eyes to dart – thus to become a little reptilian?

Chlamydia sighs in the imaginary arms of Doctor Heimlich. In her mind's eye she is being heaved from behind, hypertension physically wrenched from her body like abstract foodstuff dislodged in her craw. She coughs it up. She loves her apartment, bijou though it is. She is so very fond of her oriental carpets, the ornate wicker rocker at rested velocity beside the plump French provincial loveseat, her delicate Moroccan floral bathroom patterns and the lovely old cuckoo clock that coughs up the angry man with the raised arm and the funny moustache a bit like a Brazilian bikini wax, who comes every half hour to remind Chlamydia of old Gunter and Brunhilde set in sun-blessed retirement on the island of Morass.[1] Chlamydia's pride and joy presides on the top floor of an old converted Victorian school building. The ceilings are sharply vaulted and the walls panelled to a stiff height in morose cherry veneer. The converted bedroom boasts a cast iron fireplace with a cold granite mantelpiece and a narrow tapered alcove that spies over the old school playground – no longer host to grubby children but a prim organic vegetable patch fertilised with wholesome manure from Hackney's city farm. Chlamydia secretly indulges the harmless fantasy that this was once the headmaster's study. She can see him right now, poised rigid against the cold granite mantelpiece with a cruel fire raging in its glowing cove. It would account for the cries and whispers in the night.

[1] See *The Marriage of Reason and Squalor*, Jake Chapman, 2008.

Crowning the mantelpiece is an effeminate yet elegant watercolour depicting cosmic hurricanes spraying out into a terrible void; the space is shattered and bursts with the immeasurable force of the unimaginable upon two quaking towers. It was crafted by a clever young American artist who saw it happen and has never looked back since. Chlamydia made the triumphant purchase from one of the fashionable galleries in New York's notorious Meatpacking District. She has an instinctive penchant for modern art and relishes the modest collection of prints and minor editions she has managed to put together over the years. But such luxurious pleasures are as precarious as they are beautiful, and their tendential effect can easily wane. After all, what advantage is there in procuring stability in one's life when the only genuinely solid treasure, true love, remains ephemeral? Maybe Lomax and Sandy and Trent and her old boyfriend Algernon – and even Helmut – were right all along. It was true, she has always held men at arm's length and never really formed any purposeful relationships. In the end it didn't really matter that Algernon proved insufferable – that Trent tried too hard and that Helmut drugged her, performed a ham-fisted Caesarean and stole the infant from her womb before both infant and father disappeared from the face of the earth. The ensuing string of incompetent alliances suggested that Chlamydia had settled for an uncomplicated life and was keeping heartstrings free of unhygienic entanglements. In truth, the thought of living without love was unbearable, of existing for existence's sake in a bleak, scorch-blasted, cryo-pupeatic death-without-dying-life – and even this unpleasant string of hyphenations threads Chlamydia to the needling void that haunts her, engulfs her, swallows and spits her out into *nothingness* over again... The archaic howl neatly cross-fades with the steaming whistle shrieking in the kitchen. Even the kettle's superheated vapour fails to prevent Chlamydia from the supernatural chill that spreads through the honey-black caramelised arterial forest that is her inner-most-sickly-self. Somewhere in a lonely, petrified clearing deep in the blackest most densely forested wood, an embryonic thought: has Chlamydia Love been born cold? Nothing more than an autonomic robot, processing life's twists and turns, as grid and series, prone to an aimless horizon, without recompense for the ineluctable fact of birth, willing the onset of rust, with an aim to perish in good time. Chlamydia sprinkles a teaspoon of Kenco smooth blend into a novelty breast-shaped mug, adds boiling water to the desiccated granules and taking a wholehearted mouthful, purges the scorching liquid in a splutter of foul, unrepentant language.

A rash of keen blisters craze Chlamydia's napalmed lip. She sighs.

'No Chlamydia, you're not a silly old rusty robot; you may not be blessed with love, *but you still have pain.*'

With an uncanny telepathic sense, the telephone interrupts with the telltale sound of the outside world trying to force its way in again.

'Hello! Chlamydia, is that you?'

'Yes. It's me.'

'It's Thelonius Bell... From *The Someday Times Magazine.*'

'Hello Thelonius Bell from *The Someday Times Magazine*...'

'Is it a bad time? Don't tell me you're on yer fucking blob! I'll call back in a day or two...'

'Wait! Thelonius! Sorry! I was in a dilly daydream! Silly me! Thelonius! How are you?'

'Oh y'know. Usual. Average. Same shit, different toilet.'

Thelonius Bell is a barrow boy at heart, and ruthless media tycoon by brain. His is a typical rags to riches tale. As a favour to the corporation and its shareholders, he put *The Someday Times Magazine* back on the tabloid map. Chlamydia has a lifetime subscription backed up in her toilet because *The Someday Times* art section provides the chit to the art world's chat, and sometimes Thelonius Bell relies upon Chlamydia to pen reviews of the more taxing art exhibitions because she tells it just how it is in smaller more digestible words without dumbing down.

'Listen doll, I got a job needs doing. *Hush, hush like...*' Thelonius Bell, all urgent and throat-cancer-husky.

'What is it?' Chlamydia, all hushed.

'Word is, things are not exactly *brotherly* in the Chapman household.'

'Who? I'm not following you...'

'The artists, the Chapman brothers.'

'Oh! They've fallen out? *So what?*'

'Look! I take your point – Jesus! You're right! Fuck me! Nobody gives a shit, and it certainly ain't newsworthy, but the thing is they're supposed to be doing an exhibition at God's very own White Cube in July, and the gallery has shelled out on pricey ads all over the shop. Jopling is adamant they're still doing an exhibition, but I can't quite see how it's gonna happen if the artists ain't even speaking! If I'm honest, my motivation is simple. I wouldn't miss the opportunity to make those cunts Jopling and Marlow squirm. So I want you to interview one of the brothers. It's been organised.'

'Which one?'

'Jake Chapman. He's the only brother prepared to blab.'

'Oh, the one who dislikes journalists?'

'With a vengeance. But does he still speak to us? Indulge our little queries? *Oh yes he fucking does.* Knows which side of his bread is buttered. Gets a bit tetchy, waves his hands about, loves the sound of his own misquotes, it's all part of the act.

He gets nowhere for it. What d'you think?'

'Okay Mr Bell. How do you want it handled?'

'You handle it as you see fit, my dear – because at the end of the day he will feel handled...'

'Why me?'

'He requested you... Why? Dunno, more fool him.'

Chapter Three

From the tinted vantage of a backseat Addison Lee, Chlamydia watches as London's satellite high-rises collapse towards the godforsaken stone ruins of the west. Beyond London's congested exit she discovers the wondrous freedom of the three-lane motorway and once hitched to its escape velocity soon appreciates the unbound freedom of the countryside. In the countryside she sees thick forests and wire fences protecting baronial estates from the procession of prying eyes rolling along the undulating causeway of the M40, unravelling its asphalt tongue deep inside mother nature, scything down through the chalkstone culvert into Oxfordshire. Chlamydia sees grazing sheep and cows stalled by barbed wire. She sees mollycoddled horses, dullard donkeys and abstract roadkill littering the hard shoulder. It soon dawns upon Chlamydia that this very route leads to Aunty Shigella's stone farmhouse in the idyllic village of Carterton. Sure enough, they bypass Carterton and Witney and reach the Little Chef on the roundabout at Burford, there turning off to rudely bisect the golf course and then dipping past the Cotswold wildlife park. Aunty Shigella lives not a stone's throw from the subject of Chlamydia's journalistic safari, and to the cooing approval of the driver, the sedan makes a few twists and turns on smaller country roads before being buzzed through a wooden gate to trundle along a broken private track. As the urbane people carrier tentatively negotiates the driveway's gaping potholes, Chlamydia tumbles into her own personal black hole – the crushing singularity pulling her inexorably towards the incomprehensible fate waiting at the road's end.

Even the Chapmans' dealer, Jay Jopling, was as tight-lipped about his most cherished artists as he was voluble about their work. On the telephone he seemed keen to finesse Chlamydia's interest, was circumspect about the nature of the siblings' recent dispute and outright coquettish about discussing the future of their collaborative efforts. He refused to comment upon the rumoured schism, and when asked whether he thought it might soften the brothers' fanatical perspective and foster permission for them to perhaps even speak about feelings rather than fascism, he was afflicted by a fit of phlegmatic coughing. He was, however, unflinching in his confirmation that both Jake and Dinos Chapman were to deliver an exhibition at both branches of White Cube in July – Hoxton square and Mason's Yard. Yet Jopling offered little detail as to how the creative lacunae might materialise before rewarding his conviction. Information was scant, facts misleading.

'Jake and Dinos', he said, 'prefer to speak for themselves, individually.'

And that was that.

Gloom sets upon the garden as death sets upon the embalmer's table... livid as meat, and dense as the table itself. The farmhouse fascia hosts contorting shadows being projected by nocturnal pollinators ravaging night-blooming foliage – moths and bats, following the concentration gradient into the pungent source to gorge upon sticky laevulose. Silhouetted against a blackened sky, trees are raped naked – the chilly, damp wind blows through their emaciated cages with eerie sounds that haunt the lurching dusk. An imbecilic grimace illuminates the pathway to the front door before withdrawing into the darkness.

'Come... Come *inside*.' A voice from within.

Chlamydia makes chase through the claustrophobic

aperture into a kitchen with unexpected proportions and a glazed panorama now blighted by the blackened beyond. Chapman is nowhere to be seen. Mood lighting beyond the glass fades up to illuminate a swimming pool choked by lurid green algae. Dilapidated poolside furniture, tangled with children's toys, is strewn about the decking, alluding to some expired heyday when fun once haunted the house.

'Hello... Anyone home?' She searches the voluminous shadows for a sign of her elusive host.

'I'm here.'

'Are we alone?'

'Yes.'

'Where are your children?'

'With their mother...'

'Where is your wife?'

'With her mother...'

'Where is your dog?'

'With my father...'

'Where's your cat?'

'No idea...' And now abandoned by his brother, this is a man truly deserted.

'May I ask why I had to come here at such an hour?'

'I sleep in the day, work at night. I find the ungodly hours most rewarding for my work.'

Nosferatu pivots from shadow with an inelegant stoop craning an ungracious paunch. The face is unremarkably familiar, *but the voice...*

'It's funny, I've never had the pleasure of meeting you in person, but your voice... *I've heard it before.*' Says Chlamydia, olfactory senses quickened, but time and place retarded – strange how the olfactory senses can summon acute perceptual reminiscences whilst being devoid of the specific spatio-temporal vector in which they occurred; like 'car-crash' so wants to compress into 'carcass', Chlamydia's olfactory senses are on collision course...

'Perhaps you've heard me lecture?'

'No, definitely not.'

'Perhaps you've seen me on television?'

'Naaaa.'

'The internet?'

'Nope!'

'*CD?*'

'Don't think so!'

'You're not what I expected,' he says, in an effort to counter her damning uncertainty.

'What did you expect?' she says, all obtuse.

'Something else.' Oblique.

'You had an idea of me before you met me?'

'Yes.'

'Why?'

'Why not?'

'What was it?'

'Just something else. It doesn't matter. It makes no difference.'

'It does.'

'Why?'

'Because I want to be just what you expected.'

'But how could you be? I expected the wrong thing.'

'I want to be the wrong thing.'

'You don't want to be who you are?'

'Who am I?'

Chlamydia lunges for the light switch and the room is suddenly aflame. Chapman recoils, a snail's antennae being cruelly teased by an invasion of excess stimuli. The kitchen is strangely familiar, bubonic – steadily eating its insides-out. Human consumption is not the subject of the feast; a mist of intoxicated fruit flies gorged on fermenting fructose are hovering above a green haze describing the collapsed outline of rotten food. On the kitchen table spoiled plant stems sip on heavy water sagging in the seat of a decorative vase, stench diffused up through the crown of lifeless flowers. Naked animal bones litter the kitchen floor, circled by the stained forensic eluvium that describes the intimate process of their dismemberment. Key to the digestion process, fetid maggots link the kitchen's industrious decay in chain gangs of invaginating guts, pulsing with the selfless hard labour purposeful in returning vagrant matter back into the continuum of resurrected life. Deposited over work surface and kitchen table, bottles of rank milk reek with autopoietic potential – lipids and enzymes catalyse and emulsify with dynamic morphological transfer. Chlamydia witnesses vile biology truly expressing its multiple personality, such that the clots of matter straining to emerge from each strangled bottleneck rasps in a chorus of emphysemic tracheotomies. Added to this mess, a multifarious array of visible insectoid life-forms active in pollinating the synchronised transversal bloom – massaging the involuting scullery-organ to breathe *in and out* – gasping *in and out*…

'THE CIRCUS, THAT'S IT, THE BLOODY CIRCUS!' Chlamydia cries. 'You're *UNCLE BUNCLE!* The artist! It was you! In the tent! How funny! What a bloody coincidence! It's amazing! *But there was something quite different about you… can't quite put my finger on it…*'

'My nose. I was wearing a disguise. A prosthetic rubber nose.'

'A rubber nose? What? Why?'

'I don't like being recognised…'

'Who by?'

'I don't know. *I can explain…*'

'What has the circus got to do with this interview?'

'Don't you remember? Really? You must! In the tent, reading my palm – you were about to reveal something, but you stopped. Said you saw something, *it* was telling you – something to do with my creativity... I need to know... Especially now...'

'Are you joking?'

'No.'

'You're serious.'

'Deadly. I haven't been able to put it out of my mind. By sheer fate I happened across an article on that mad old batty French artist, Louise Bourgeois – there was a thumbnail portrait of you next to it. I recognised you and was astonished by the coincidence. I had no idea that you also wrote about art. After that I was compelled to speak with you. I had to meet you – and then the opportunity arose because of the exhibition coming up in July at White Cube. The two things seemed to marry... align...'

'Okay. Let me explain. I'm not clairvoyant in the slightest. To be honest, I couldn't tell which day of the week it is at best of times. I was merely standing in for a friend, Maman Ewe, the *real* fortune teller. I was doing her a favour because she was poorly.'

'Maman Ewe?'

'Yes. Maman Ewe *is* Maman Poisson.'

'If Maman Ewe is Maman Poisson – who are *you?*'

'Chlamydia Love. I write. I'm a writer. Remember?'

'So you were faking?'

'Excuse me Pinocchio! You're the one with the perjurious rubber nose!'

'It's my disguise!'

'I thought it best let that one go –'

With the unique expression of an infant unfairly scorned,

Chapman's lower lip quivers.

'I think there's been a bit of a mix up...' says Chlamydia, only slightly smirking.

'OH I GET IT! YOU DON'T HAVE SUPERNATURAL POWERS AT ALL! YOU BLOODY CHARLATAN! IMPOSTOR! YOU DON'T KNOW ANYTHING ABOUT THE FUTURE – OR THE FUTURE OF MY CREATIVE WORK! IT WAS POINTLESS YOU COMING HERE! AND ANYWAY, IF YOU ACTUALLY HAD ANY POWERS OF CLAIRVOYANCE YOU'D HAVE KNOWN NOT TO BOTHER AND SAVED US BOTH THE INDIGNITY OF EACH OTHER'S COMPANY!'

And with that, Uncle Buncle ignites a disdainful sneer and evaporates.

For a while Chlamydia is rooted to sheer disbelief. When Chapman fails to rectify his tantrum she decides to chance her luck by calling out to the far reaches of the house, appealing to her absconded host to return, but receiving nothing for the trouble.

In the kitchen she fiddles with stale finger food before boredom decides to brave the hallway and discover the vaulted living room. She discovers the television and turns it on, hoping the sound of strange voices might draw out her timorous interviewee. So she sits patiently on the couch grazing with the proviso that if Chapman fails to materialise after reasonable time, dignity will be forced to abandon the interview, phone Aunty Shigella or a local minicab and flee to Paddington via Swindon on the next available train. Sat on the couch next to her is a book – a well-thumbed and substantial novel lying face down. She turns it over. *Cained and Disabled*, the latest bestseller by... *Helmut Mandragorass, Chlamydia's erstwhile man-friend, the man who drugged her and performed a hobbyist Caesarean and stole the unborn infant from her womb before both creatures effectively disappeared from the face of the earth. So Helmut is alive and writing – but what of Chlamydia's son?*

Sitting comfortably, she begins...

Cained and Disabled
by Helmut Mandragorass

I

From the depths of the first almighty shriek a nascent yell prematurely unfurls, but it is the infant's postpartum howl that tears so keenly at the hairs on the hunter's nape. He scours the lovely green chlorophyll tangle, keen imagination conjuring a wounded beast, yet instinct tells him the scream does not belong to any creature of the forest. Like a sleepwalker drawn towards self-harm he edges closer to the noise with arms outstretched. But as he nears, the sound withers, reduced to a drawn harmonic whine – the morbid death-knell that sucks life back into the archaic big bang from whence it came – *incomprehensible howl of God's first fuck*. It would be at least humane to help it on its way to meet its maker – would also make a welcome change from stale pig brawn and stagnant cabbage water. So the boy weaves from tree to tree and soon reaches the edge of the forest to find that the sobbing comes from beyond the forest edge, where the valley dips towards the river. There, out in the open, under the raging sun and beyond the cool rein of the forest, he finds the woman with skirt hitched above waist and bare legs cruelly twisted apart. He sees her distended belly – the sad navel ready to rasp like a birthday balloon. He stares at the mewling creature wallowing in the soil of its murderous discharge. He stares at the vein and gristle braided together, tethering the runt to the ruptured hole from whence it came. He gazes at the mother's spent flesh and is so moved to drop his own litter of skinned rabbits to the ground. Thus cut down to grazed knees he finds the girl blue with cold, luminous face rinsed of life. He shakes her shoulder to wake her up from his dream but instead a porcelain breast falls loose. Then tearing at the linen, ripping the shirt wide apart to contemplate the squandered bloom before him – the squandered protein, and lifting the mewling creature onto her bosom he regains his feet to observe at full height as the imp blindly nuzzles for its dead mother's milk like an uprooted mole dazzled by sunlight. He observes it suckle hopelessly, gulping air like the fish he allows to drown beneath the merciless sun. Thus he beams down upon the pitiful bundle of nerves before him and is so moved to heave at the sight of its unnerving lust for life, its mortal instinct – the blissful insignificance weighing down upon its splendid and obscene struggle. To marry mouth to teat he first nudges the creature with gnarled boot, then with filthy fingers only to find the umbilical leash will not allow it. He tugs on the cord but cannot extend its length enough to couple mouth to gland. Beyond reach of the gulping jaws a perfect ivory bead weeps from nipple, sags momentarily before its glistening meniscus collapses and a tear of milk cascades to waste in a fold upon the corpse. He unsheathes his blade, wipes rabbit blood in a coagulated crease ground into his sleeve, only hesitates for a moment before cutting the cord close to the bellowing runt. Darkest fluid drools from the severed ends like oil from the brake cable of the Baron's jet black Mercedes, so tying a crude knot in the flex, he lifts the creature up in his arms and rises to his feet. With his boot, he shoves the woman's knees together, turns and abandons the three flayed leverets to perish alongside poor Snow White.

In the glaucous snarl of the forest, the image of that which has been abandoned soon catches up with him. As he clambers back through the thicket he finds himself entertained by proxy of an imaginary wanderer come face-to-face with the profane composition he has left behind. The wanderer is choked at the sight of the tragic young waif succumbed in child labour to the bloody brood laying flayed next to her – obscene speculations foam into the empty space that the imagination permits, conjuring the moment of taxonomic blasphemy – the sight of *Daddy*, an enormous *oryctolagus cuniculus*, his fur engorged with criminal love, fluffy white cottontail bobbin nailing human flesh into loam, both beasts lapsing back into nature... a single yelp of boyish laughter escapes out into the murderous-shitty-world where it belongs – before involuntary morbid joy is tamed by tense rictus grin. He thus presses the creature into his ribs deliberately and continues for home. To the wailing infant he whispers – *your daddy was a wabbit, and your three sisters are all dead*.

As usual Mummy is in the kitchen expecting her son to arrive with food enough for the family of eight. Sometimes he would manage a chicken, some eggs or steal cigarettes from the Baron's supermarket where his father toiled for a pittance. Or sometimes, when times were especially good, clutching KFC buckets like a squalid pig farmer he came home having purchased a Family Feast® to feed the whole family on twelve pieces of savoury factory-farm chicken, four servings of French fries, a family tub of congealed baked-beans, coleslaw and a bottle of tepid Pepsi. But this evening was anything but a KFC party night. He nudged the bungalow door with the toe of his boot and there, in the gloom offered the fruit of his earnest predation to the eager scrutiny of his hungry mother.

Mother's instinct first draws a claw to breast and for a moment the woman can only gaze at the wretched sight before her.

'*What is that?*' Her granite face softens. 'A baby boy... Where did you find the poor little thing?'

'Out in the open. Down by the river.'

'And its Mama?'

'Cold as a witch's tit!'

A cursory hand swipes the boy's face before falling upon her own body to softly genuflect for her sins whilst shivering to the softest marrow of most superstitious bones – wan face, drawn frown, the sum composition of outward serenity subcutaneously betrayed by the ferocious skeletal smile baring its grinning teeth beneath the compliant skin, silently laughing its skull off.

'Quickly now, run and find Daddy. Find him! Tell him! ... Tell him what has happened. *Now run!*'

Gladly rid of the rancid mite he wipes its filth upon his trousers and runs to find his father to tell his foul tale. Mummy shoves the door shut with a razor hip, yells for her eldest to fill the kettle, then perches on a stool, unbuttons herself and coaxes a tired nipple to the gulping hunger belching foul air in her lap. Tiny-Tears, her youngest, must go hungry tonight. For that matter, so will the whole family.

'And for what?' she says aloud, eyes mooning up into cumulus lids, tucking the child into her nook. 'Poor little bastard, you'll be dead as a doornail by the morning. We'll bury you in the garden and no-one will care about your passing.'

As though preparing for its journey into the frostbitten ground, that night the local midwife came and bathed the creature and tended to the angry umbilical stump erupting from its deathly white flesh. Daddy seemed struck by an unwelcome optimism for the child's chances and stood by in silent observation whilst contemplating the unwelcome burden of new life upon the mountain of endless sufferance and shit that already weighs down upon his weary spine.

'When a guest comes into the house, God comes with them,' declares the sage old hag, adding, 'tis a shame about his poor, useless, hopeless legs... Poor soul!'

'*Soul?*' Daddy spits, 'this *soul* to which you so confidently refer, this *spirit* or *inner essence* is merely an abortion gestated in the pit of the stomach, simply biding its time and awaiting release by maggots! Merely a dyspeptic ulcer cradling the necrotic substance of its irritation – life, dear woman, is irritation! And anyway, look around you – we've enough jackanapes of our own to feed without incurring the nuisance of a good-for-nothing cripple!'

Ignoring Daddy's outburst, Mummy strokes the strange net of dark filaments streaking the baby's tender cranium.

'What shall we call him?' Mummy goads Daddy.

Daddy's brittle spine hunches ready to snap with cartilaginous rage.

'Call him what you like! I say we put him out on the doorstep – let the strays look after their own – either that or they can rip him to pieces for all I care! Let Mother Nature decide...'

II

In the manner of an Aztec priest standing atop the Great Pyramid of Tenochtitlan, the Sunbelle General Hospital's resident obstetrician lifts the pulsing gobbet of flesh high in the air before slapping it hard to release the first aerobic yell from its delicate little lung. Another brat seamlessly c-sectioned into the ranks of the fiscal elite without so much as a whimper from mummy whose grossly dilated retinas still remain pinned to infinity whilst the newborn is whisked away, washed and weighed before being returned and planted back in Mummy's cosmic embrace.

Outside the delivery room an executive banking gentleman paces the corridor like a prison guard hankering for crime. Inside the delivery room two extra obstetricians have been hired-in to lend their eyes to the procedure because the father-to-be is not taking any risks. As the elected obstetrician diligently huffs and puffs away at the business end of his patient, the two supervisors offer preverbal grunts of encouragement – the farcical feature of their superfluous presence privately fortified by the fact that their perspiring associate is wearing an evening suit wilting beneath his surgical gown on account of a thwarted invitation to a society dinner party. The three physicians had thus earlier drawn straws to decide whose hands would get sullied, up to the elbow in human muck – and Shipman drew the short straw. Hurrah for Doctor Shipman!

Shipman... Now there's a name... A seaworthy moniker for sure – a perfectly good name for a son. Self-exiled from the vulgar obscenity of birth, instead to pace the disinfected corridor, the Daddy-to-be is sensitising himself to something of profound significance to leap out and claim the name of his offspring – but what could be more appropriate than honouring the man who wrenched the brat from its hidey hole? And so he paces up and down and considers the merit of this idea.

Others might confuse his pacing as a sign of concern for a loved one's labour, but he has no especial reason to fret since all is arranged far in advance. Mr Mitoku had been primed with the task of delivering Isabelle to the hospital in the family car on the twenty-eighth morning of her ninth month. Labour had commenced promptly after breakfast – once Isabelle was suitably replete, following a routine of orange juice, salmon balls, broiled mutton chops, omelette, Swiss cheese, toast and marmalade and a bowl of Earl Grey. When finished, she set her cutlery down, punctuated both corners of her coquettish simper with a starched napkin, allowing amniotic waters to fully drain upon the Turkoman rug before folding the tainted linen and setting it upon the table and uttering the command:

'Mr Mitoku. Fetch my shawl. I believe I am succumbing.'

The hospital had made every assurance that the happy event would not take place anytime before the building society had shut up shop for the day, and hence the building society's money counted, serial numbers logged, bound and stacked safely away overnight in the time-locked Schwab Class 350-1 vault, well before the baby's head appeared at the top of the cervix or before uterine contractions got stronger or before the infant was forcibly shunted down the vagina, being encouraged by contractions of the abdominal muscles and the mother's strenuous pushing. This model had been thoroughly tested at the Braunschneggerweigger Technical Laboratory by the Institute for Endurance Materials, following a rigorous set of endurance tests which commence with the placing of the safe in a red hot furnace and holding it at a constant temperature of 2000°F for fifteen minutes or so. Then the safe is withdrawn from the furnace, hoisted to a height of thirty feet and dropped to the ground. It is allowed to cool before being reheated in the furnace for another fifteen minutes before cooling naturally, and is then opened and inspected for damage. In the morning, at a specified time, the bank's safe doors will open, the money withdrawn, counted, serial numbers logged and returned by drib and drab into the lint-lined pockets of the bank's beholden, paying for the privilege of resting assured in the confidence that extraordinary measures have been taken to ensure the safety of their hard earned money.

With such vexation clogging his own progress, our man continues to pace the corridor – impatient for his beloved's time-locked vault to be heaved open and its precious contents thus revealed. Nurses, doctors, patients and visitors pass by with sympathetic smiles that blur into callous snarls as they disappear from his view – most know that if God wills this man a son, *an heir*, he might be so moved to allow his family's bank to underwrite finance for the children's wing that Sunbelle General Hospital could not afford – but could not afford to not have. This conviction is founded upon the theory that genes are the building blocks of all life, and that the proud city of Weatherfield had already so far been graced with a handsome sandstone library and a pretty red-brick school erected by the man's grandfather to memorialise each hereditary coming-into-being of his individual spawn. Hence, the theory of inheritance was deeply embedded in the Weatherfield fiscal breech.

The man takes a newspaper from his briefcase, shakes it open in an effort to divert himself from the fact that it had to be a boy, because the corporate mantle demanded it – demanded an heir to one day become president of the bank like his father had been and his father's father. Further back he didn't rightly know. The sanguine start to the year is now a distant memory as the appetite for risky assets wane. Spreads were already widening this week amid fears that a shift in China's monetary policy could choke off any further growth. Matthew Muller sang Eminem while brutally stabbing each and every member of his entire whole family in Kansas. He told police that he sang Eminem songs while fatally stabbing his wife and daughter. His four-year-old son survived the vicious attack, despite being stabbed a total of eleven times. Muller said he was possessed and believed his wife was a demon. Just before stabbing her at four a.m., he told police he started screaming lyrics from an Eminem song, shouting, 'Here comes Satan, I'm the anti-Christ, I'm going to kill you!' Muller told police that when his children awoke to their mother's screams, he stabbed them too. He said he stabbed his son Joseph the most because he loved him the most. The delivery room door's rubber fringe snags open on a curling tile. Doctor Shipman emerges in pantomime evening dress, black tie and holding a large Cuban cigar given to him by one of his sly associates, now held out before him as though handing on the baton of humanity to the next sucker in line. So taken aback by the physician's surreal change of costume, Daddy wonders whether this casual celebration is entirely appropriate and begins to hum, *Here comes Satan, I'm the anti-Christ, I'm going to kill you!*

'Congratulations sir, you have a child, a healthy baby, a fine little *boy!*'

III

With everyone else tucked up in bed, Carrie Hoffman remains astonished by the bleating orphan in her arms, yet she cannot help but haunt herself with anguished recollections of the two little ones successively taken from her in childbirth. On the other handy-pandy she considers how brutal life is for the surviving six and for a brief moment contemplates strangling or drowning the orphan to save everyone the fucking bother. Now at thirty-five, her husband Yuri knows not to trouble her special place with greedy pleasures that invariably lead to hungry mouths. She was grey and thin, worn out by the gravity of a heavy hand-to-mouth subsistence. With a customary sigh she squeezes her ragged breast so hard that a dull red mark ornaments the flesh circling the nipple.

'Little one, don't fret,' she whispers whilst prompting it to suckle. So she sits patiently, until sleep draws over her like an embalmer's shroud, slumped forward, enveloping the infant in the safe carcass of her grey, worn thin frame.

Yuri Hoffman is a dull man with a full black moustache – a pitiful gesture of emasculated sovereignty set against the relentless labour that would one day break his back. Rising before dawn, he stumbles into the kitchen half-asleep to discover his absent other-half cradling the orphan in the rocking chair. He observes them as they slumber, gathers his keys and some stale bread, and like a man whose very soul is possessed by the conviction that he would only ever earn final respite by working himself to death – dissolves into the choked black forest.

Eldest child Pocahontas skulks into the kitchen around six to prepare breakfast. She is frail – a scrawny little thing whose fair hair shines and hazel eyes sparkle in defiance of the poverty that tarnishes any hint of youthful luminosity. Craning over the rocking chair she can not resist stealing the orphan from her mother's limp arms to cradle the newcomer in her own – but the change in temperature and scent disturbs the infant from autonomic aestivation and so triggers it to yell blue fucking murder.

'Jesus wept!' mother shrieks, 'I can't believe he actually survived the whole night!' She snatches the child onto her breast. 'Pocahontas! Make breakfast for the boys while I feed the little one!'

'Feed the little one! Feed the little one!' shouts Pocahontas, drunk as a honeybee knee-deep in pollen.

When Daddy returns home that evening with six and a half mushrooms and three modest potatoes to add to his son's seven stale donuts, the Hoffman family sat down to a veritable feast. After supper, Daddy slumps in the rocking chair near to the gas fire and takes time to study the child properly. Held at arms length the infant is wrinkled and toothless. Its legs are hopelessly limp and useless – its only redeeming feature being the fine, blue eyes – yet to find focus somewhere beyond the kaleidoscopic abstraction.

'Have you noticed this?' says Daddy, prodding the baby's chest roughly. 'The little bastard has only one nipple! Mononipple!'

'Don't curse! He is a gift from God,' says Mama. 'It's *His* mark.'

Daddy thrusts the child at Mama. 'You sad old fool! The louse who begot this specimen already spoiled its mother with bad blood. *Bad blood I tell you!*'

The gas fire hisses with Daddy's spittle.

As the days passed Yuri Hoffman came to terms with the fact that the concentrated efforts of his telepathic malice gnawing away at the orphan's head was unlikely to make it go away. Eldest son Gideon fashioned a cot from twigs while Pocahontas cut little pieces from her old dresses and sewed them together for clothes. They would have called the little bastard Harlequin if they had known such a word derived from the black emissary of the devil, who roamed the countryside with a cohort of demons to chase the damned souls back to Hell. In truth, naming the orphan caused more disagreement in the Hoffman family than just about anything else, and so the consensus settled upon the name *Helmut*. Sure enough the child was soon christened Helmut Hoffman.

IV

Isabelle had slept as sound as a baby. After breakfast, her newborn son is fetched in the capable arms of a barren maternity nurse who pounds the corridor as though her ice-cold vagina dentata is doing the cha-cha-cha. Mommy can't wait to hold baby again.

'Your son,' says the starched nurse crisply, 'it's time to give your son his breakfast. He is hungry. Look see how hungry he is.'

Isabelle sits up aghast by her own rudely swollen breasts. The nurse offers instruction on how to feed while Isabelle feeds, mother dissolved into son's ice blue eyes, more distantly gelid even than his father's. She smiles all content and so does the little one. At twenty-one, she wants for nothing else. Isabelle chatters to the hungry maw as it suckles itself to milky oblivion. When the child is drunk with milky love his glacial eyes melt everything in a narcissistic mulch, only then does Matron take him away to sleep off his milky coma.

Little Helmut Hoffman grew with such glacial timidity that it became evident that ill health would beset him until the blossom of his dying day. Even the sickest of illnesses and diseases spent time convalescing in his hypogammaglobulinemia before setting off to hard work on the rest of the family. Carrie treated Helmut like one of her own, defended him from the vile outbursts of her malevolent husband, who when simple rage and complex alcohols coalesced, would see fit to blame him for the universal blight of the earth. As for poor Pocahontas, she took care of Helmut as if he were her very own illegitimate pre-teenage love child. Eclipsed by endemic poverty, Helmut represented Pocahontas's only ray of hope. Eldest brother, Gideon, the little cunt who had inadvertently rescued Helmut from the deranged taxonomic rapist rabbit, either treated Helmut like a mere plaything, a damaged rag doll or simply shunned the frail weakling. The three younger brothers, Arthur, Bobby and Jamie, similarly showed little interest in Helmut's injurious existence, while the remaining member of the family, baby Tiny-Tears was only six months and so cherished any opportunity to cuddle, suck and scratch on naked flesh she could get her oral/anal suckers on. So the physical and cerebral differentials were glaring. The Hoffman children were tall with rust-red hair and manual labour ingrained in their eyes. Condemned to the floor, Helmut was nonetheless short in length. He had dark hair and blue eyes. As for education, the Hoffmans had no purpose for it and customarily abandoned village school as soon as necessity demanded their blood, sweat and tears. Helmut did his best to turn frailty to an advantage and was able to speak at twelve months, read before his third birthday and write elegant sentences at five. As for Helmut's bowels and bladder, they were beyond education, a rule unto themselves. Incontinence made him the scourge of his father and the apple of his mother's parsimonious Christian eye.

Helmut's first four years on earth were hell. He dragged his sorry soul around the wooden bungalow dressed in a worn orange jumpsuit, always a yard or so behind his mother, numb legs split like sausages and knees riddled with splinters and abscessing sores. When sister Pocahontas returned from school each day he followed her like a sad puppy soliciting simple contact from an alien species. Pocahontas often sacrificed her food to the weakling, taught him songs and shared the few toys in her possession. When Helmut was old enough Pocahontas pulled him along in an old log-fetching cart through the dark woods to the little school in the village. Helmut loved school. It was an escape from the bungalow that had until then been his entire world. Mr Dopey, the schoolteacher, did not try to beat Helmut's spirit into the ground like his father did at home and so he soon graduated to the top of his class in everything except woodwork and height. At night, while the other children tended the violets that bloomed so fragrantly in their springtime garden, or picked red and black and blue berries, or chopped wood, or teased delirious myxomotosis rabbits, Helmut read until he was blue in the face – read books until he was consuming adult literature stolen from his guardian's shelf.

So it dawned upon Carrie Hoffman that she had taken on more than she had bargained on that fateful day Gideon returned with the crippled creature in lieu of din-dins, abandoning the three yummy leverets to perish with their adopted dead mother. Precocious Helmut soon began cross-questioning his mother about his birth and why he was so unlike his sisters and brothers. Whilst she deflected his interrogations as best she could, she prayed that he would one day find enough comfort in her love and cease speculation.

One autumn evening the family shared beetroot soup and diced rabbit. Father was stewing by the gas fire and Mummy was knitting while the children were watching dear Chucky on TV with dead eyes and dead hearts. Helmut was stooped at the feet of his mother, softly buttressed against her firm shin with a well-thumbed book. There was a determined knock, knock, knock on the door. The Hoffmans fell silent. Visitors were rare. Yuri snapped from his dogmatic slumber, growled across to the door and yanked it open with aggressive aplomb. At the sight of the visitor each of the Hoffmans cowered and bowed their heads – except silly Helmut, who, nun-the-wiser peered directly up at the noble silhouette draped in a heavy coat.

Helmut deferred to his father and for the first time

witnessed genuine fear bleach into his Father's own murderous eyes. Father stepped aside to permit Baron Mandragorass' entry. Nobody dared speak except Chucky who was stabbing, gouging and stamping. Helmut dropped his book, the pages fluttering over the spine with a literal sigh. With strangely determined intuition, crawls towards the stranger's leg, grabbed his trousers and pulled himself up far enough to catch the stranger's eye.

'Hello. Who might you be?'

The Baron cranes over and pats the cripple on his head with something approaching bona fide affection.

'Zo! You must be ze Helmut.'

'Yes I must!' replies the cripple gaily, unperturbed by the Baron's unaccountable familiarity.

'Zo you are ze reason I have come here zo to visit ze father of zis... *home*,' says Baron Mandragorass. Yuri waves the other children away and they disappear like rats scurrying into the recesses of a humble sewer. Helmut remains glued to the spot.

'Hoffman,' commences the Baron, 'I have ze big fat favour to ask of you.'

'A favour? From me sir? You require a favour from me? Me? Anything, sir, anything I can do I will do, anything for you...'

'Haben Sie eine Induktionsschleife für Schwerhörige? Zo! My son Nemo is now ze six years old, ja? Unt right zis minute is being tutored by ze two tutor-mentors at ze castle, ja? One ist hailing from ze land of ze gypsies – zis is ze Poland, ja? Ze other from ze Fatherland but I think more from ze Motherland, if you see what I mean, ja? Zo! Zey tell me zat he is bright but lacks ze concentration... ze conviction, ja? Zo zis is far from ze superdanke! Zis is ze unterdanke! Ja? You follow me? Teacher Dopey in ze village schools informs me zat Helmut is ze only pupil he knows zat is capable of providing my Nemo with ze companionship and ze encouragement he needs unt zo I have come to ask you if you permit your son to leave ze village idiot school unt join Nemo unt ze one-to-one tutors at ze castle.'

Helmut summons up images of endless shelves of beautiful gilded Teutonic antique books amassed in a wise old library reeking of a thousand Reich-long year wisdom, but cut short, the like of which he had once read about in a book he got from the village school library before it burnt down. He was tired of his teacher's provincial sagacity and glances up at mother. Mother's face is tinged with sorrow. Sorrow is pallid grey. Father turns to mother, the moment of insipid telepathy between them lasts a virtual eternity in the manner that pain is drawn out in torture – suffice it to say, Helmut can plainly see it is Mummy being tortured by Daddy.

'We would be so very honoured, sir.' Daddy gestures with his hand toward Helmut.

'The Blessed Virgin Mary Magdalene, patron saint of sexually and mentally abused children, forbids that I stand in my child's way,' said Mummy softly, 'but Lord Jesus H Christ alone knows how much I'll sorely miss the little mite.'

'Be assured, Madam Hoffman, ze Helmut may return home whenever he has ze wishes to do so. My God in zis place mir tut der Kopf weh!'

Madam Hoffman bows her head.

'Zo. Zis is settled zen. Bring him to ze big castle tomorrow morning. During ze term time he will live in ze big castle – but at ze idiotic Christmas time when ze Christians play at generosity with ze giving of ze unwanted gifts – zen he may return unt you will be welcome to the little Schwienehund.' Helmut bursts into tears of happiness, his tears of joy shrewdly camouflaged by the very same tears of utter dejection and sadness.

'Quiet, you thankless little shit! We've looked after you for as long as we can – we can't afford any more operations! No more! Now it's up to someone else to sort you out!' says Daddy, agitated on the surface but happy just below.

'I shan't go!' Helmut yelps, turning to his mother with imploring eyes that can't help plead with her to let him go. Everyone is lying. Sulphurous odour wafts up from numerous gut sutures cross-hatching Helmut's body and have aggravated his nostrils for so long that an amorphous mass of compensatory scar tissue has erupted from the place where a sneering nose has sniffed itself in permanent disgust.

'Enough!' says Daddy.

'Welche Einrichtungen haben Sie für Behinderte? Nothing! Haben Sie Toiletten für Behinderte? Nein danke! Haben Sie Zimmer im Erdgeschoß? No! Haben Sie einen Aufzug? Nein! I very much doubt it! Haben Sie Rampen für Rollstühle? Clearly ziz is not zo! Wo ist der Eingang für Rollstuhlfahrer? Eh? Where? Nowhere! Ja? Zo why do you wish to stay here – in zis filthy hovel where ze father clearly hates ze guts? Ja?' asked the Baron, with potential compassion in his voice.

'Because I don't want to leave my sister – *never!*'

'Ich nich lich? *Sister?*' queries the Baron.

'My eldest daughter, sir,' says Daddy. 'Don't worry yourself with her, sir. The little bastard cripple will do as he is fucking-well told.'

The Baron studies Helmut as he flails helpless on the tiles, break-dancing like a squirrel with a broken back, I know because I've seen one in real life.

'What is ze name of zis... eldest daughter?' he says.

'Pocahontas. *After ze film...*' says Daddy, blushing.

'My God! Die Waren wurden beim Transport beschädigt! How *old* is zis Pocahontas wet-back nigger half-breed?' he quizzes graciously.

'Fourteen going on forty,' says Daddy, his smutty eyebrows up and down.

'Is she proficient in *ze... kitchen?* Can she... *cook?* Wash up? Clean?' asks the Baron.

'Oh, yes, Baron,' Mummy responds. 'Pocahontas can... cook... sew... wash... iron... dust... fetch... cash... carry...'

'Good... good... zen she can come as well. I shall expect both tomorrow morning at ze seven-on-ze-dot. Ja?'

Behind the rainbow waterfall of inhuman tears Helmut smiles.

Before beddy-bye-byes Mummy packs for Helmut and Pocahontas. In the morning the others stand by the door and watch as the two hand-plucked children depart for their new improved life in the Baron's Mandragorasscastle. During their departure Pocahontas is elegant and graceful, glancing backwards and waving to her folk as she drags Helmut propped up in the battered wood cart. Helmut never once looked back.

Helmut and Pocahontas are clearly expected by the manservant adorned in an elaborate embroidery suit skilfully mocking the diminutive stature of his station, who answers their timid knock on the great oak door of Mandragorasscastle with a grin spanning from ear to there. Inside the door a heavy woven rug laps the length of the hall like a prolapsed tongue blossoming with pretty halitosis. Helmut stares at its charming green-and-red rash, stunned by its epic beauty unfurling before his very eyes. Indeed, he wonders if he should drag his corpse around the outer edge instead over the carpet. Thus encouraged forward by the servile dwarf, he is pleasantly surprised that when crawling over the woven path, his sores cause him little-to-no pain.

They are conducted to their separate chambers housed in the eastern wing and once unpacked of beleaguered possessions, which amounts to nothing at all, Pocahontas is whisked away to the hellish scullery while Helmut is dragged to a playroom in the south wing where he is to be introduced to the Baron's son Nemo Mandragorass who is tall for his age; a fine blue-blooded specimen only lightly tainted by consanguineous genes, and yet is so very charming and uncomplicated that Helmut feels instantly at home in the Baron's big castle. Helmut senses Nemo is a lonely child with no one to play with except his BoBoo, the devoted slave-cum-nanny Lithuanian who has selflessly suckled him and attended to his every rinse of shit since his Mummy's descent into insanity and eventual suicide.

Thus in one matter at least they are equals.

Nemo towed Helmut around the castle in a silk pillowcase taken from his father's bed whilst Helmut delighted at the sheer magnitude and vast opulence of the medieval structure. Nemo tells Helmut how his daddy's castle is of the 'French Style'.

'I suspected as much!' Helmut pipes up. 'I've seen pictures of Gothic architecture in picture books!'

Nemo bumps his new friend down a stone staircase into the immense cellars, where row upon row of wine bottles lay doused in dust and sticky cobweb. But Helmut's favourite room of all is the enormous dining hall, with its massive pillared vaulting, flagged floor and possibly the largest table in the world. He gazes at the menagerie of trophy heads mounted on the walls, the angry bison, the irritated bear, the furious elk, the wild boar and the ill-tempered wolverine – exotic creatures from esoteric lands falling foul of the taxidermist's stuffing. Above the fireplace is a brass coat of arms announcing the Mandragorass family motto:

Glück ist bloß ein plätzchen mit einer Nachricht innen
[Fortune is just a cookie with a message inside]

At noon, a terrifying claxon echoes through the stony medieval labyrinth announcing lunch to be served by quaking servants dressed in humble dinner lady uniform. Helmut is bewildered by the array of silver cutlery and is at a loss as to its purpose and so manages to ingest very little. After lunch he is introduced to his two tutors, who greet him with studious scorn. That evening he rests upon his bed and relays his escapades to his exhausted Pocahontas who remains bravely transfixed throughout, soothing the luminous blisters on her fingertips with dabs of spittle. Lessons began before breakfast the very next morning and continued throughout the day, with only short breaks for sustenance. Like this the days and months pass and Nemo and Helmut find healthy rivalry in their work and the comfort of companionship in their play. Their mentor's dogged reluctance eventually gives way to effervescent praise and duly concedes to the Baron's pedagogic gamble. To wit, the Baron is most pleased with the boys' progress and sees fit to reward little Helmut with items of clothing, educational toys and books. But when the first snows of December begin to dapple the castle gardens, Helmut succumbs to a seasonal blanket depression. He feigns happiness on returning home for Christmas and puts on a brave face when Mummy drags him around the Arndale Centre Christmas shopping – at least the floor is polished and static electricity minimal. As the season of goodwill edges towards its holy zenith, Helmut feels overcrowded and hemmed-in. He longs for the freedom of the Mandragorass castle and knows in his heart of hearts that the Hoffman Bungalow will never again be home.

In Helmut's absence, Yuri's profound hatred of his adoptive

son has merely fermented, becoming more pernicious – especially now, confronted with a debonair six-year-old boy with an eloquent tongue, silky manners to match and a conversational range to confound his erstwhile guardian. Yuri Hoffman took it upon himself to sacrifice the family pet kitten and pray to Beelzebub and the legion of the damned that Christmas pass quickly and the brat be returned.

Carrie Hoffman is so proud of how grown up her little boy Helmut is. But as is often the case, things are not as they seemed. Christmas day descends like an embalmer's shroud... solid as livid meat on a morgue slab, dense as the slab itself. The bungalow is tangled with cheap tinsel and the voices of angels congest the air. In the corner of the room a cheery coniferous boasts Baron mandragorass' trickle-down charity lurking beneath the shade of its pine needles – a brightly wrapped present for each and every member of the Hoffman family. Gathered around the pagan token, Daddy fetches the gifts from beneath the tree, shaking each before handing it to its excited recipient.

'Ah! *Mummy*... I think this one is for you!' Mummy takes the present gingerly, gives it a customary shake and perfunctory listen. She unwraps, paying especial attention to avoid unmasking the Cellotape too efficiently and preferring instead to tear through the colourful paper like a demented child.

'Oh! A beautiful, *beautiful* handbag! Why thank you *Father Christmas!*' Her eyes wide with holy appreciation, she shrugs and coos until Daddy's big paw reaches beneath the tree to retrieve the next parcel.

'Ah! *Pocahontas*... it's for you!' says Daddy, the giver of gifts.

Soon, Tiny-Tears has unwrapped her pram and Pocahontas has unwrapped her Canon PowerShot A480, and Arthur has unwrapped his Sony DVPFX730 portable DVD player, and Bobby his Nintendo DS, and Jamie his Sony PSP. The luck of the draw would have it that only Helmut and Daddy are left. Daddy reaches and redeems a modest package.

'Ah! ... For me!' The giver of gifts.

Daddy unwraps a box of finest boutique premium cigars and takes time to savour the smell of the balsa box before cracking its seal. Inside, the cigars are jammed next to each other like slaves in a coffin. He levers one of the cigars from its brethren and slowly drags it along his moustache to savour the earthy, leathery undertones, the hint of mild spices, cedar and cocoa – all the while keeping an eye on Helmut. Daddy snips the cigar's end and lights the obscene protuberance.

'Mmm... smooooooooooth...'

Through the digital cacophony of camera jingles, flashes and swirling smoke Helmut sits patiently, but he can see nothing in the shadows beneath the Christmas tree and so his heart sinks.

'*Silly boy!*' says Daddy, 'you didn't think we'd forget you? Did you?' Daddy has a brand new face that Helmut has never witnessed. Daddy reaches far into the shadows beneath the Christmas tree.

'For you. *Dearest son*. From all of us...' says Daddy, visibly elated, almost ecstatic.

The farewell chime of Canon, Sony and Nintendo switching off prompts Mummy to pipe up.

'*It's all we could afford...*' she says, with nervous eyes darting to and fro between Daddy and Helmut, like two tiny fruit flies fearful of the human palm. Helmut takes receipt of the small round object, cradling its preciousness in the cup of his hand. He notices the shoddy newspaper enveloping its round form but prefers himself to think nothing of it.

'Golly gosh! What could it possibly be I wonder?' he says.

'Open it! Open it!' cries Tiny-Tears, jumping up and down. Helmut unwraps the first layer of newspaper. As the second layer falls loose he sets eyes upon the soil-smitten onion. Yuri Hoffman can't contain the glee that sniggers from behind his shovel hand. Helmut continues unwrapping the onion. First he picks off the brittle skin, then the first inner green layer, and then the second and third, and so on. At the seventh layer he pauses and looks up from studying his Christmas gift. Tiny-Tears is transfixed, keen to see what is inside, Carrie and Pocahontas are both afflicted by helpless tears, but Gideon, Arthur, Bobby, Jamie and Yuri Hoffman are gaping with utter astonishment. Holding the onion's anaemic cellophane heart up to the light, Helmut chirps –

'Why thank you! Dear family! One should always know one's *allium cepa* and this is certainly a resplendent specimen! Organically cultivated in accordance with the Soil Association I presume?'

Daddy can manage nothing audible. Only Gideon is so moved to speak.

'Well... in any case, you're not really our brother,' he blurts. There is a painful silence before Gideon adds, 'It's true! We never wanted you here in the first place – Mummy allowed you to stay because she felt sorry for you!'

It was left to Pocahontas to disclose the details of Helmut's humble origins, and she did so while towing him in his wooden cart back to Mandragorasscastle the very next day.

•   •   •   •   •

Thus the unforeseen lure having the power to eventually draw Chapman from his absent sulk is the sound of Chlamydia's grief-stricken sorrow – her unrepentant weeping, the unmitigated wailing, the excruciating howl emitted with each turn of *Cained and Disabled*'s onerous page. She wonders how such a tale about a drug addict son of a millionaire banker and a crippled orphan can turn out, but a baritone cough announces Chapman's prodigal return, the apparent metempsychosis is marked by a stark alteration in appearance, since now he is dressed in brown leather cowboy boots, spray on jeans and a dark shirt; a wide black belt with a brass buckle depicting a pretty Staffordshire bull terrier propped above lean hips. Broad shoulders strain the very fabric of the shirt; top buttons are relieved of the duty of being fastened and the almighty column of his neck is exposed, tanned, muscular and latticed with a glut of proud veins. Jake's expression is softened by the dissipative quality of the ambient mood lighting plus the thick black curls tumbling over his forehead like a hairy waterfall.

'Come...' he beckons. 'Freshen up in the guest room... *if you like*.' Curiosity follows dutifully, kneading the tears from its eyes like a lost child.

'I was only crying because I lost my... May I borrow this book?'

'In there... *Enjoy*.'

He cleaves the wide door with effortless ease, strides back down the hallway, a tall, lithe figure with the broadest shoulders and captive wild animal grace. Chlamydia takes a moment to sit on the edge of the bed, still wrapped in coat and beret. The room is decorated brilliant white; a plump eiderdown suffused with black animal hair smothers the divan. Two harlequin patterned side-tables stand guard either side of the bed with an en suite to the side cleverly disguised behind a sliding door. It is surely breathtaking, if not a little Spartan, but Chlamydia is in no mood for an unpaid critique of the interior decor on account of still reeling from the revelation that the disreputable Uncle Buncle of the circus turns out to be none-other than artist Jake Chapman plus Helmut Mandragorass has written and published a best seller and there's not so much of a hint about the whereabouts of her stolen offspring.

Oh well. I'm sure he'll turn up in another book – perhaps a best-selling sequel to *The Marriage of Reason and Squalor*? Who knows? So much for fortune telling.

A. Removing coat, (B) beret, c. jumper, [d] watch, E shoe, f) Chlamydia poses a few off-the-cuff questions, Q) Why would a man who elects to preserve his identity from the public by wearing a ludicrous prosthetic nose suddenly see fit to reveal all? (1) It didn't make much sense that so vain a man would expose himself for the sake of a public he so customarily spurned. 4) Resignation shrugs its shoulders and decides to take a shower. To wit: (-5-) Solving Jake Chapman was going to require the crispest mental fortitude, and (6). Chlamydia, like most -7- women, needed to feel at her best when confronting such an inherently treacherous male of the species, if only to present him with the moronic reflection of his leering gaze, oblivious of the jeopardy it puts him in. There is no time to ponder such trivialities, and so, with an unholy rub-a-dub she is no-sooner cleansed back to default freshness.

In the kitchen Chlamydia is greeted amicably, although keenly ushered to the large sliding kitchen door, where artist ushers critic from the house into the pitch black where inferredness triggers an incandescent halogen to scorch the route to a large stealthy building embedded in solid darkness. Pure sculptural brawn manoeuvres colossal doors whilst Chlamydia prepares to take her first step into the breach of the creative domain. When the master switch is thrown on the motherboard, Chlamydia's astonishment lights up like Christmas. Ceiling floodlights ignite a space so vast that she is quite sure it would easily engulf an entire ladies' netball court. The walls are adorned with big and small paintings plus preparatory sketches for paintings yet to be painted. The floors are a dark bare wood and the room is roughly divided in two parts. One part pristine white, where finished paintings hang according to strict gallery conditions – individually lit, enjoying ample space for the artist to appreciate their singular intensity without their individual intensity being compromised by the morass of intense canvases littered about the place. Everywhere, wooden stretchers are stacked against walls. A vast table with all terrain rubber wheels is laden with a spectral rainbow of oil paints and mixing pots sprouting sable or hog hair brushes, waiting to be plucked by the artist's numinous hand. Above the very dead centre of the studio a skylight presides in the manner of an enormous all-seeing evil eye beaming down on human creation. Chlamydia can see for herself that this is one man's singular vision – nothing attributable to Chapman's collaborative oeuvre.

'It's simply breathtaking!' she yelps, jumping up and down. 'I love it! I love it! It's a triumph! *Bravo!*'

'Not another word!' he protests, yet wilfully soaking up Chlamydia's radiant first-impressions – the artist's ravenous aureole glowing, all engorged and pulsating dangerously such that Chlamydia is fearful of the consequences of overfeeding the meter – as if to confirm her fears, a surge of alter-egoic electricity arcs between them; burns her forearm through the polyester fabric of her dress, rages like wildfire through the conductive core of her prime-beef marrow. Fully charged, the critic jump-starts into motion, fizzes and sparks, goose-stepping along the cohort of paintings set uniformly along the wall, stopping to examine each for a second or two before marching off to inspect the next. Truly, Maman Poisson's forestalled clairvoyance on that fateful night possessed more prophetic charge than the fake fortune teller gave credit –

something is up with Chapman's creativity, but even the predictive powers of the most supernaturally gifted would fail to anticipate what lies in store...

Here, an image of a wizened old man, lined and angular, bearing witness to a young girl with sad, old, eyes, capturing that unique and fragile moment when childhood blossoms into adolescence and twilight beckons for Granddad. Hanging on the studio wall, an unemployed banker pleads for loose change whilst diffident workers pass on their way to work off the interest on ill-advised greedy loans. Elsewhere, a vile-faced wench stares down at the spectre of her own seven-toe'd feet, and a small boy with webb'd fingers and two heads beseeches his dysphoric mistress from the quagmire of the canvas' lower left bank quadrant. Some of the pictures are cruelly obliterated by scribble or crossed out, emphatically vandalised by obdurate rage, whilst other pieces have managed to survive the artist's editorial savagery.

Everywhere, tumescent eyes gripe with a disquieting pathos, not satisfied with following you around the room, but drilling into the core of your very being.

'But why painting? Why now?' she says. Dictaphone alert.

'Because I was sick and tired of all the clever books, the *discourse*, the crippling *critique*, the idle *chitchat* and the incessant *blah-blah-blah*. I came to realise how I was trapped inside this impermeable bubble of self-doubt and despair – impounded by a synthetic *idea* of art rather than being invigorated by its active process – stifled by the hideous social intimacy of the art world. I wanted to do something *real* and just for *me* for once. So I moved my family to the Cotswolds. I woke up and I smelled the roses – I even decided to paint them...' He gestures to a small canvas tucked behind a chair and ornamented by a small jar of wild roses tentatively rendered in substandard oil.

'So this is what you've done for the show at the White Cube gallery in July of this year – and these paintings are your *personal* contribution to an ostensibly collaborative Jake *and* Dinos Chapman exhibition. I don't quite understand how that works...' Chlamydia is straight for the jugular, in for the kill.

'No.'

'No? You're not showing these at White Cube in July?'

'No.' The artist's craggy fascia sheers a sly granite fissure.

'Please explain...'

'These are the *preamble*. They have delivered me to my true *métier*.' He gestures with a ventriloquist's directional nod to the far corner of the studio where a cluster of wooden easels stand loosely covered with protective dustsheets.

'Can I?'

'You can.'

Chlamydia lifts the plastic skirting up and ducks under to find herself face-to-face with the first easel painting. Eyes, brain, and mouth are thrown into a blind swivet, seeking escape in all directions before conjoining neural elasticity snaps them back into the ontological discomfort of the existential aggregate to which they belong. Chlamydia emits an uncouth yelp. A compromised quizzical frown seeks tutelage in the artist, and receives exactly nothing but the ambivalence of a man truly rinsed of explanation. Salacious curiosity stumbles further inside the trompe l'oeil brood, beneath the plastic umbrella and propelled by odd utterances of non-verbal astonishment, the critic undertakes a haphazard internal inspection, staggering from easel to easel inside the translucent amniotic bubble of impermeable self-doubt like a tapeworm measuring a gut – or a botfly larvae seeking the miracle of illumination through it's host's ruptured eye... Chapman watches the embryonic sac forming soft abstract shapes with elbow and hand as the occupant's infantile and half-baked love of art proceeds inexorably to the moment of traumatic rebirth. All is going well, until poor Chlamydia clips one of the easel's feet and looses her balance. Understandably, her reflex is to grab at the nearest upright to steady herself, but unfortunately the chosen upright is lamentably unstable and can offer nothing more than a loose pole for Chlamydia to swing around, thus coming face-to-face with the next shocking image, the traumatic sight of which merely adds to the sum total of her physiological imbalance. Simple panic elects to grab the painting to seek resistance to an inelegant cascade, but the said canvas – itself merely leaning upon the easel as support – offers no resistance at all to the critic's now clumsy critical mass – so she tips, falls, flails, buckles, tumbles, crashing to the floor. In a courageous but retrospectively injudicious attempt to protect the dislodged canvas, Chlamydia has failed to release it from rigid clutch – and on being re-born into the studio from the polythene uterus, presents the fallen painting before her, a masterfully expressionistic likeness of an impudent muse reclining apathetically on an unmade bed, tangled in the midst of dishevelled sheets, one languid arm raised above his head, the other hanging loosely over the edge. The handsome devil is pictured with an irascible, unseaworthy smile and the entire piece being tinged a lurid green to match his uncouth sentiment. Unfortunately, Chlamydia's head is now a semi-permanent feature of the work, and penetrates the painted surface of the canvas from the reverse, fouling the area where the sitter's proud genitals once sat in the seat of their erstwhile glory.

'Look! It's your brother Dinos! *He's all nude...*' says Chlamydia, seeking sanctuary in stating the obvious. 'They're all of your brother Dinos... *all nude!*' Chlamydia struggles like a rabbit clenched in a nasty snare, staring up at the foul-faced farmer bearing down with subsidised malice. 'I'm so, so, so sorry! P-p-please help me free myself. I promise to pay for the restoration...'

'Don't fret,' says Chapman, 'there's plenty more where that one came from.' He gestures easily to the phalanx of canvases propped against the heavy-duty crate hand-crafted for imminent export and then sets about easing the painting from its blathering obstruction.

'I just want to say, for the record, that these pictures are the most courageous paintings I've seen in ages. I'm absolutely gobsmacked, speechless and lost for words! You've really pushed the boat out this time, and all on your own! You're going to stun the critics to silence and set the art world on fire. Imagine! Forget all those other dumb schmucks of your generation! This is the real deal! Don't get me wrong – some people won't get it. They just won't, and don't ask me why – it's just the way it is. It'll take time for some to catch up – but mark my words, they will, they'll soon catch up, because they'll have to – it's the way of the world, see? But the people who do get it will really get it, straight away – like a shot! Bang! Right between the eyes! Bullseye! I'm telling you... it's a complete and utter U-turn without falling prey to Academician YBA/OAP dementia! You've even liberated yourself from all that Sensation Saatchi mind-control bullshit!'

'You're trembling,' he says.

'Am I?'

'Yes.'

Chlamydia searches for something to fend his looming gape from hers. So the jilted journalist rises from dogmatic slumber to its defence –

'Is this your permanent residence?'

Closing in, until mouth forcefully docks with hers, his and her lips are at now one, one long invaginated alimentary canal full of shit and spittle – his tongue is compelling, forceful. She weaves her wings around his nape to tangle fingers in burnished black strands of long dark hair. His hand runs down her back, clenches body to its unspoken demand, arching slim form to match breasts pressing against chest, the line of thigh running along muscular leg, sweeping through like a hot, molten leak. But then he unexpectedly parts company, moves away, disengages, leaving Chlamydia gaping like a trout out of water, lips all luminous and engorged and gagging. Just then, the enraged studio floodlights dim significantly. In the half-light Chapman is palpably angered. He hurls himself into the human-sized hamster-wheel that poor Chlamydia had until now assumed was an impressive and satirical sculpture satirising the Protestant Work Ethic Inc. But no, the fine artist is now sprinting his heart out to feed the dynamo to which the overhead lights, and perhaps the house (and freezer) are dependent. Full luminosity is soon restored after the artist's blistering calorific burn and so he slows to a more aerobically manageable jog.

'The Nazis in your work – are you trying to evoke something of *Entartete Kunst?*' says Chlamydia.

'Entartete what?' he pants, hands on hips, puffing.

'The Nazi art exhibition – Degenerate Art.'

'Oh Yes. That. Yes, I am. Yes.'

'Why?'

'Because who else better to pin the blame on than the Nazis, the transcendent baddies, evil ad-infinitum. It's their fault... always their fault, forever and ever, Amen. Just like Jesus. Like Jesus died for our sins, the Nazis live on for our evil. The Nazis excavate our fascism... *sublime from sub-slime...*'

The light is beginning to dim, so Chapman picks up pace.

'But why does your work have to be so... *pessimistic?*'

'Pessimism is also funny, no? *Sufficiently funny – deadly funny.*' Chapman is jogging.

'But why so morbid?'

'What? Speak up!' Chapman is running.

'I don't see why it all has to be so unpleasant for the viewer.'

'Can't hear! Can't hear you!' Chapman is near flat out.

'YOU COULD HARDLY SAY YOU WORK WAS INTROSPECTIVE!' she yells.

An expression of earnest puzzlement compels him to stop running –

'INTROSPASTIC?' he asks, but the hamster-wheel continues spinning, thus propelling the artist violently onto his still-quizzical frown. Chlamydia can do nothing but laugh out loud at the sight of the artist tumbling about like a soiled rag doll in the cylinder before crawling on all fours from the contraption once it has slowed to humane full stop.

'Right! You bloody asked for it!'

‡   m
··"<?%?íµy?ä??xxxÜJFQ°ÏU¢∂≤iÙDsÕ~8Á¡‹ÿÿÖ@A$Yò"}y
ñv1ú‰&µÎí;I‚n﹡-u/¢t()mD°„‹'Âí?k9MÄ›(é§??yQ? +U˘†-
iò8ÕÉ   j¡çßÖò3oY?Jâ}?rI1?ïÖµ{?VyQ? +U˘†-iò8ÕÉ
j¡çßÖò3oY?Jâ}?rI1?ïÖµ{?VyQ? +U˘†-iò8ÕÉ
j¡çßÖò3oY?Jâ}?rI1?ïÖµ{?VxÖ)ZÏêçr(w)¥Åg«?EqöhC"?=hí
ÂÒA‡uQ?   ‡²ÌØ-(a)rc()Í•£OH?+àøù@'k-Õ??'?d&È'e
MP†AL(mtÌ)?6µç?±Xø÷ï(µmtr)(5)cÑ≤..m.,ì≠îè!ä†?e¿∂?Ó?4
]èÌCëbÈ÷ïIöc(X)vJR?êú/£d?egCô5îú?&4ïq'??›°"gâ?l?m??ü·.f
. . ` % e ? ¥ y < † y Q ?   + U ˘ † - i ò 8 Õ É
j ¡ ç ß Ö ò 3 o Y ? J â } ? r I 1 ? ï Ö µ { ? V r (I) Ò r (-
)≤?°Ô ? 3Â?$?9L°B›ºªç???x#?^`)ã lçÚ"SÅ°∑√EÙ} ;flesh felt
taut over an internal shape made likely for an epidermis of
greater surface area, plus where thinner skin was directly
supported by bone, it glistened with a tensile pressure showing
the burnished silicone could rupture plus the spring-loaded

bone fly out in all direction, the collective anxiety clenching the hospital held that the broad surgical Chelsea-smile on the leader's face had the latent threat of an anti-personnel mine:-9U¨'z5'È,ˇM?&?AUÕQ?ÅÕ??ready   to

detonatevV?~Àl±Ja÷5??skin splitting plus skull bursting out an hitting you on the head and maybe knocking you out forever- one grin stretched too far or a laugh too structurally demanding....

..`&≠Ø2?!`N≠e«Óí?ñI_]?>AëÜ¿Dï+fõ(ü)c-Òdoyou see? ?aª@y•°6ø??b1ù!û each embroidered neatly snug as a duclotic bug in a rug, stapled from ear to there, pock-ridden moon-scape gurgled drowning pores, capillary oil-wells wait in turn to vomit sub-cutaneous puss-contents between the grubby fingernails of a lover's squeezing digitsâ

Á°??XD out an hitting you on the head and maybe knocking you out forever-&≠Ø2?!`N≠e«Óí?ñI_]?>AëÜ¿Dï+fõ(ü)c-Ònow do you see?Á°??XD?ˇ∂?ˇ∂Yô2éÃ?∑

q+8v›xã¥_=]∆ÒÚÆÑu??%   Q⁻Ìëãïa-S??]n??Vá_ù?r-?-*'K» È?ùMMíµA?ÏÔA skull scything outwards into the astonished flesh of anyone unfortunate enough to be beholding this exponential head in its moment of terminal velocity, while fluttering, sensitive insect like, top plus bottom eyelids adorned with deadly tarantula spiders that caressed each other when blinking   shut,   ?kru?V≠??8C±ÂÑî5-?D.»..U¥≠N?6![Ú around herr eye balls, ãeÓXh?ªK~≠?okö??4xÛ?ãNôÖ??acute nocturnal laboratory hours etched deep into the

patina;?(qK?›úBâúKm#?Ç·%¸???yúÒ_???pQs&^U:"li'äïÕ;·?
¡^±*ÖZË>Yóï'}e+ ..1.¢Xµ   -µIx-ˇzå° black concentric
rings circled drowning squid-ink eye-wells plus spiralled deep
into dreadful smeared toilet-hole retinas,   ›VÂ??9,/- plus
when herr tranquil face became overdrawn with ragey black
clouds, herr eyes vanished altogether beneath hydraulic flexing
of herr heavy mantle brow plus right on top of this soiled
plateau your grandma could plant her entire photographic
family-tree of loved-ones with room to spare for any new-born
cheesy   paedo-
smiles.›"?d∂ñ??S)B'çà>:ÅäcÜEÁ≤?Ù?Í=Z|?Ò>jóu!?
· ‰ f Ì ÷ µ ú a ? ? : •] ? D ? é û ä ù ≠ ¶ â -
¬'›'8?âÈµÍHMz:3A?ÀÚ?¥?????w8I±¡ÕÁ#5*?..O.
?o}≠÷›.!k}?e⁄?
???
????? Evaporative surfaces herniated by the sun suffer
exothermic ruptures,
??fissuringradon and blocked background radioactive cells
enveloped in structures coerced into tranquillity ?baked int
disruptive contortion as the sun's carcinogenic avalanche
tortures???
???
???
???
???
???
???
???
???

???
???
???
???
???
???
???
???
???
???
???
???
???
???
???
???
???
???
???
???
???
???
???
???
???
???
???
???
???
???
?????????????????????something trying to force its way into
o   u   r
world???????≠???

? ? ? ? ? ? ? ? ? ? ? ? ? ? ? ? ? ?
???????????????????????±?????????????????????????????
???
???
? ? ? ? ? ? ? ? ? ? ? ? ? ? ? ? ? ?
□□
□□
□□
□□
□□
□□
□□□□□□□□□□□□□□□□□□□□□□□□□□□□□ the sec?nd d??r ellicits
a crude br?wn c?lumn as wide as a tr?R?man ?? ee-trunk that
rises-up like a stimulated catapiller, this time irritated, scowling
brown smears of contempt, punching through the flinching
laminate security glass, impacting upon its wire grid as it
implodes into splinters and squares. red cloth. Poised alongside
was a sad skinny girl wrapped in an anorexic feather boa
and defoliated sequin swimsuit to match.??? □   □ Ú   0
□   □ Ú   0   □   □ Ú   0   □   □ Ú   0
□   □ Ú   0   □   □ Ú   0   □   □ Ú   0
□   □ Ú   0   □   □ Ú   0   □   □ Ú   0
□   □ Ú   0   □   □ Ú   0   □   □ Ú   0
□   □ Ú   prurient   express
□□
□□
□□
□□
□□
□□□?□□□
□□
□□
□□

□□
□□
□□
□□
□□
□□
□□
□□
□□
□□
□□□$3 $3 $3 $3
@   "9   ä/   ä/ $3 $3   Ó2 6 "9   "9   "9
$3 ?? ä/ $3   ä/ $3   ,?   "9   û/ r ?0 r ä/
ä/   ä/   ä/ $3   ,?   "9 ¿? "6   ,?   ä/   ä/
,?   ,2 Tn`? ∂1 ? ¬2   "9   ,?   ,? $[$[
,?   ?_   "9   ?_   ,?   "9
??
????????ù????¢ ˘□@ ˘□   ä/ $3 $3 $3
$3 $3   @   "9   ä/   ä/ $3 $3   Ó2 6 "9   "9
"9 $3   □□ ä/ $3   ä/ $3
,□??
?????????????????????????????????ha ha ha ha ha ha ha ha???4
9 4 9 5 9 5 9 5 9 6 9 6 9 6 9 7 9 7 9 7 9 8 9 8 9 8 9 9 9 9 9 9 10 0
1 0 0 1 0 0 1 0 1 1 0 1 1 0 1 1 0 2 1 0 2 1 0 2 1 0 3 1 0 3 1 0 3 1 0
4 1 0 4 1 0 4 1 0 5 1 0 5 1 0 5 1 0 6 1 0 6 1 0 6 1 0 7 1 0 7 1 0 7 1 0 8
1 0 8 2 1 1 2 1 1 2 1 1 3 1 1 3 1 1 3 1 1 4 1 1 4 1 1 4 1 1 5 1 1 5 1 1 5
1 1 6 1 1 6 1 1 6 1 1 7 1 1 7 1 1 7 1 1 8 1 1 8 1 1 8 1 1 9 1 1 9 1 1 9 1
2 0 3 1 3 3 1 3 4 1 3 4 1 3 4 1 3 5 1 3 5 1 3 5 1 3 6 1 3 6 1 3 6 1 3 7 1
3 7 1 3 7 1 3 8 1 3 8 1 3 8 1 3 9 1 3 9 1 3 9 1 4 0 1 4 0 1 4 0 1 4 1 1 4
1 1 4 1 1 4 2 1 4 2 1 4 2 1 4 3 1 4 3 1 4 3 1 4 4 1 4 4 1 4 4 1 4 5 1 4 5
1 4 5 1 4 6 1 4 6 1 4 6 1 4 7 2 0 1 9 1 9 1 9 2 0 2 0 2 0 1 4 7 1 4 7
1 4 7 1 4 8 1 4 8 1 4 8 1 4 9 1 4 9 1 4 9 1 5 0 1 5 0 1 5 0 1 5 1 1 5 1 1

5   1   1   5   2   1   5   2   1???????????????????
??
???o?????????
???????? She came up to me, changing her grip on the stick
as if ready to thrash me across the face with it, diseased by the
active conclusion that leads towards terminal pathos
characterised by symptomatic??????????????irrigations and
congealing aggregates –, here, in this very domain, being
becomes ill enough to be diagnosed human, and most protein
of all -being is entirely prone a peculiar gesture of the neck,
deliberately forcing her injury on me. She paused when she
reached the doorway, waiting for me to step out of her
wayWith the nasolabial fold this new line formed fate that
remains, despite its epistemological enthusiasm, absolutely
unthinkable. Doubtless any eschatological resolution
represents a wish-riddled myth happily doomed to catastrophic
collapse –' Bellowed Fuckface, eyes popping and vein-latticed
head winding forward on its taut trunk while sub-
blasphemouslaughterclimaxed his convexed cheek. 'Dip-shit!
Dip-shit! Daddy is   Dip-shit! Daddy is   □□□□ÿ □
□□□□□□à□□□□□□□□àÅ□□ □□ Å□□□□□□□□□□□□□□ □□□ Ä
Äò 0   0   Ä Äò 0   Ä Äò 0 Ä Äò 0 Ä
Äò 0Ä Äò 0   Ä Äò 0   Ä Äò 0   Ä Äò 0
Ä Äò 0   Ä Äò 0   Ä Äò 0   Ä Äò 0   Ä
Äò 0   Ä Äò 0   Ä Äò 0   Ä Äò 0   Ä Äò
0   Ä Äò 0   Ä Äò 0   Ä Äò 0   Ä Ä0 Ä
Äò 0   Ä Äò 0   Ä Äò 0   Ä Äò 0   Ä Äò
0   Ä Äò 0   Ä Äò 0   Ä Äò 0   Ä Äò 0
Ä Äò 0   Ä Äò 0   Ä Äò 0   Ä Äò 0   Ä
Äò 0   Ä Äò 0   Ä Äò 0   Ä Äò 0   Ä Äò
0   Ä Äò 0   Ä Äò 0   Ä Äò 0   Ä Äò 0
Ä Äò 0   Ä Äò 0   Ä Äò 0   Ä Äò 0   Ä
Äò 0   Ä Äò 0   Ä Äò 0   Ä Äò 0   Ä Äò

0　Ä Äò 0　Ä Äò 0　Ä Äò 0　Ä Äò 0
Ha!' Bellowed Fuckface, eyes popping and vein-latticed head
winding　forward　on　its　taut　trunk　while　sub-
blasphemouslaughterclimaxed his convexed cheek. 'Dip-shit!
Dip-shit! Ä Äò 0　Ä Äò 0　Ä Äò 0　Ä Äò
0　Ä Äò 0　Ä Äò 0　Ä Äò 0　Ä Äò 0
Ä Äò 0　Ä Äò 0　Ä Äò 0　Ä Äò 0　Ä
Äò 0　Ä Äò 0　Ä Äò 0　Ä Äò 0　Ä Äò
0　Ä Äò 0　Ä Äò 0　Ä Äò 0　Ä Äò 0
Ä Äò 0　Ä Äò 0　Ä Äò 0　Ä Äò 0　Ä
Äò 0　Ä Äò 0　Ä Äò 0　Ä Äò 0　Ä Äò
0　Ä Äò 0　Ä Äò 0　Ä Äò 00　Ä Äò 0
Ä Äò 0　Ä Äò 0　Ä Äò 0　Ä Äò 0　Ä
Äò 0　Ä Äò 0　Ä Äò 0　Ä Äò 0　Ä Äò
0　Ä Äò 0　Ä Äò 0　Ä Äò 0　Ä Äò 0
Ä Äò 0 Switch-cells
 z???? ?? ? drugged head Fuckface????fed inside ?ribbed
Vagerox cavity ????server-drone　　?　　z??? ?? ?
?big red button mushrooming from ? enamel surface Ä Äò
0　Ä Äò 0　Ä Äò 0　Ä Äò 0　Ä Äò 0
Ä Äò 0　Ä Äò 0　Ä Äò 0　Ä Äò 0　Ä
Äò 0　Ä Äò 0?　Ä Äò 0　Ä Äò 0　Ä Äò
0　Ä Äò 0　Ä Äò 0　Ä Äò? 0　Ä Äò 0
Ä Äò 0　Ä Äò 0　Ä Äò 0　Ä Äò 0　Ä
Äò 0　Ä Äò 0　Ä Äò 0　Ä Äò? 0　Ä Äò
0　Ä Äò 0　Ä Äò 0?　Ä Äò 0　Ä Äò 0
Ä Äò 0??　Ä　　　?　? Ú　　0　　　??????
? Ú　　0　　　?　? Ú　　0　　　?　? Ú　　0
?　? Ú　　0　　　?　? Ú　　0　　　?　? Ú
0　　?　? Ú　　0　　?　? Ú　　0　　　?
?----the human disease Ú　　0　　　?　?
Ú　　0 ?　? Ú　　0 an image like the palm-lines of a
sensitive and elusive hand. Reading an imaginary biography

into this history of the skin,   ?   ?Ú   0   ?
?Ú   ?   ?Ú   0   ?   ?Ú   0
?   ?Ú   0?   ?Ú   0   ?   ?Ú   0
?   ?Ú   0   ?   ----   is as fo
llows:::?   ?Ú   0   ?   ?Ú   0
ington - ?'   0   ?   ?Ú   0   ?   ?
Ú   0   ?   ?Ú   00   ---   t
he surplus effect of the death-drive
?   ?Ú   0?   ?Ú   0   ?   ?Ú
0   ?   ?Ú   0   ?   ?Ú   0   ?
?Ú   0   ---allows truth to re-emerg
e syringed inside a glowing open-ready ulcer on lower left
cheek, Not unduely z??? ??   ?upset by the colonization of
his veins   ?   ???? vampire clones   ??$?   ?
reddening of the skin Äò   0intelligent life   Ä   Äò   0   Ä
Äò   0   emerges to competeÄ   Äò   0   Ä   Äò   0   Ä
Äò   0   0in the accursed share of morbid introspection,   Ä
Äò   0   Ä   Ä0   Ä . My wishes are: a humble cottage
with a thatched roof, but a good bed, good food, ^ í^ õ^)_
0_ z_ Ü_ ¶_ Ø_ ¿` ...` Éa èa ?a ‰a >b Jb c c [c hcthe
freshest milk and butter, flowers before my window, and a few
fine trees before my door; and if God wants to make my
happiness I M M 'N O $O ,O _O dO íR ñR ãW ìW
Y Y FY SY ¯Y Z :[@[›[‰o[æ\ «\ Á\ Ù\ @] G] ›]
^ {^ Ñcomplete, he will grant me the joy of seeing six or seven
of my enemies hanging from those trees. Before their death I
shall, moved in my heart, forgive them all the wrong they did
me in ^ í^ õ^)_ 0_ z_ Ü_ ¶_ Ø_ ¿` ...` Éa èa ?a ‰a
>b Jb c c [c hctheir lifetime. One must, it is true, forgive
one's enemies - but not before they have been HANGED'. i
ê? ersonal fossil scars and perjurH2Ofi
brillosedelicate winged Ferrisbabies. G
enome streams and gism-encapsulated7

Ʒif convertible, ˇ? ? ˇ? ! ˇ? " ˇ? # ˇ $ ˇ % ,} & îq 'We (
Y) Proffessor Heimlich's easter island head appearded
brandishing a hyperdermic.'There, you've had your fun, now
back to business'. The syringe swelled as it came towards
him until the point was so large that Fuckface realised it was
entering his eye. With a pop and a sigh Fuckface said 'hello
hell'. Entropy = a system's capacity to evolve irreversibly in
time, and the degree of randomness ho was largely helpless but
endearing. 'Praise the Lord!' ho -nail jabs thsings the black
crack-addict atheist security guard.'Your welcome!' shruggs
prostitute-made-good Nurse smiles swipe across their such
vertical speed that the stuccato glockenspiel begins to palpitate
and then flatline into a single uninterupted tone. A The
swingdoo????????????à?? † (r) ˇ? ? ˇ? ? Word
'Microsoft @ "9 ä/ ?ÿ ?Sixor disorder in a system,
entropy tends to increase in an isolated system. A parental
smile too friendly by far. A m C S †zô ?˜T †zô ?˜U †zô ?˜V
†zô ?˜W his from hers. The second leant close to Fuckface
jabbing him with the cattleprod to spark the words 'I "9 "9
$3 ?? `^ ¢ ˇ?@ ˇ? Ó2 6 "9
? ? ?? Å??????àÅ?? ?? ?????0 r ä/ ä/ ä/ ä9
? √ ? Âä/ $3 ,? "9 û/ r ? ä/ $3
$LOVE YOU MUMMY AND DADDY' ? written on the cue
and now flaring from his mouth j captured cocktail of proteins
and nucleic acids to organise into living physiology: eventually
cities †zô ?˜X †zô ?˜Y †zô ?˜Z †zô ?˜[†zô ?˜\ †zô ?˜]
†zô the ?? ? r ?0 r ä/ ä/ ä/ ä/ $3 ,? "9
¿? "9 ,? ä/ ä/ ,?
,2 Tn`? ∂1 ? ¬2 "9 ,? ,? $[$[,?
?_ "9 ?_ ,? "9 ? √
? Â? ? ? ? ? ??? z ?? ??
exchange
embedded deep in ? hermit hillside too hot ??? ?

z Citizen
donated food from way inside his Mall
where ? whole town lived???   ?nt an exploding cigar ?
????? ?   ?
?a mind you
creaming off ? tip of a buttermountain and ? other peaks in
his surplus food stockpile.

.

        Vicodine%??? Gamma& a pneumatic ???'???
vapour(???)condensation system ??? leaking prismic sc???
all   over   the
shopI???J???KKKClonazepam,laminar+???,???reverb-
panic2???3????4???5???6hydraulicdelivery-???intravenous.
????/???0???1???Diazepam   ???7???
Valium8???9???:???;???<??? Benztropine, =???>???????
@???A???B)Lithium???C???DDoxyelectro-
chemicallamine???E??????G???H??? L???M???N???
O???P???Q???R???S???TTrimethobenzamidessssssssstatic
and frenetic$??? Vicodine%??? ????????????tight-lipped
mouth-gut-anus volume-sensitive gastrointestinal flue or bile
hydrant, ?????????anus exit entry,pneumatic ???' mouth
hypersensitive to broadband interphage voices ???
vapour(???)condensation system ???leaking prismic ???cs all
over   the
shopI???J???KKKClonazepam,laminar+???,???reverb-
panic2???3???shelllike earache laps with oceanic tsunami
tide 4???5???6hydraulicdelivery-???intravenous.???/???0
non-referential craters of libidinal energy ???1??? Diazepam
???7???   Valium8???9???:???;???<??? Benztropine,
=???>??????? @???A???B)Lithium???C???DDoxyelectro-
escapehatches make access ready for predictable code-crash
spilling across fixed unities bleeding into no-man's land
chemicallamine???E???G???H???L???M???N???

O???P???Q???R???S???TTrimethobenzamivolume-sensitive gastrointestinal flue or bile hydrant, () anus exit entry,pneumatic ???' mouth ultrahypersensitive to broadband interphage voices ??? vapour(???)condensation system???leaking prismic ??? ???J???KKKClonazepam,laminar+??????reverb-panic2???3??? was? ????????????? ? ? ? ? ? ? ??You better tell me,causenow he's after me!' ???U???V He was a filthy c h I l d killer... he wasgoing to get us by killing all our kids.. ? ? ? ? ? W? ? ? ? ? ? ? ??There were all those men X here were all those men X Nancy, even your father oh yes, even him. □□□□Y□□□□Z□□□□[□□□□\□□□□]□□ □ □ □ □ □ □ □ □□V□a□l□u□x□□□□□□□□□□□□¯□·□□□Æ□Ï□Ù□ã□í□÷□Å□□□Ï□□ □□□Ø□□□∏□œ□⁄□fl□□□ˆ□ê□□□□□□□□□□□□□□□□□□□□□□□□□ □□□□□□□□□□□□□□□□□□□□□□□Ar of

Aö

B? the rottenEarth

D,

HÆ

HΔ

HË

HÙ

IÇ

IÑ

MM

M§

M?
N°
N»
Q⁕
Q6
Sñ
S?
Xå
X¶
_|
_ú
ié
m¿
n
t,
u

uub	limbs,		busy		with
on		hand		and	knee
hominids	dragged		sensitive		hides
from		the		Dark	Ages
drawn		by		the	seductive
outside-in.			skinned		insane

???+if?+thiiiiiiiine?+eyes?+offend?+thee?

?□□□
  □   □   □   □   □
□□
  □   □   □   □   □   □   □   □
□□
□□
□□
□□

□□
□□]□□□□□□□□□□
□□□
□□□□□□□□□□□□□□□□□□□□□□□□□□□□□□□□□□□□□□□ñ□□□□□□□□□□□
□□□
□□□□□□□□□□□□□□

??????????????+pluck?+them?+out!?+?????????????????
??√ÿÓ　　　　™　　⁻　　√ÿÓ b { ™　　　　™　　　　　　　□
™　　　　x L # (　　X
?
?????the?+man?+with?+the?+x-ray?+eyes?+does,
?+but?+not?+before?+he?+sees?+the+end+of+the+world+
relaxes its clench?????????????????????9?????
??$?
　?

Above the lift axis as curious putrescence squeezes through;
the door rotates chops through the sludge like an emasculating
blade the bisection precipitates a violent reactionpatient's
attention-span duely contracted and found his roll-on beady
eye sliding from the card　?clone suspension is swiftly syringed
inside a glowing open-ready ulcer on lower left cheek, Not
unduely ??z??? ?upset by the colonization of his veins
?　　　???? vampire clones　　??$?　? ? reddening of the
skin signal irritated capillary-wells Fuckface frowns all
afternoon Frequent itches and echoing with the microsibling
Fuckface cells basking close to nuisances off perforating the
tedium of a long experimental day entertained by o Fuckface
melts only to find dreamscapes overpopulated by a chaoscopic
vision of miniature Halloween orphans spilling across clenched
tight plasma red firelit eyelids,the surface to attract his attention
or exit in pinprick sweat droplets nurse makes frequent visits
with a witchazel swab soon sees these ccaisional visits from

data-sipping hunter gatherers swapping Fuckface pleasantries when his cardiogram remains consistently in love with life narcolepsed protean processions of dammed voodoo effigies dancing across the mouth of the cave ink jet shadows pulling in and out of pixelation hydovented eddying Fuckface cells spiralling upwards in curling fractal hydrodynamic/smoke spat from ringed volcanic underwater pustules erupting on scar-tissue skinhead, billowing up from nowhere to go drift aimless and wait for antibiotic evacuation kamikaze stem cells quick unpicking the tissues of the knitted dreamshape weaving integrated geodesic patterns that tessellate and slide beneath Mummy and Daddy's jelly sandals dissolved by torrents of Fuckface acid raindrops falling on their steaming burning heads screaming interference at every strata collapse an electron micropornoscope's tactless probe staring at a beady nucleus, the beady eye eye-ing up the noumenal monochrome ghost mite lurking minute on a huge tapering polyhuman hair bursting through the cerise quilted epidermis, patent black rubber monsters dusted-white as molecular aristocracy nanomite-fops, scatterlogical debris wrecked all around rubble rubbish X-ray black and white wireframe, subsequent multiplication blink and the micropornological eye pierces in on the mite's mite lurking on the mite's mite's filament of hair sprouting from a mite's lateral leg panning a micrometer to the side to see the faceted hexagonal black meladome eye eyesight drone blackened dead, thrust in again mite's mite's mite's bug's eye, again, eye-ing the mite's mite's mite's mite's eye black hole retinal exchange the rest of the day slips by without injury until the military rep arrives in force to cheque its investment was budget well spent. waking him with an explosion of acetic acid. 'we're here because you're here.' An accusatory pause synchronizes the melodrama. Patinated Shark-eyes etched with close-quarter first hand excoriation and burnished stare inflects the volatile switch current of blind rage/harrowing compassion sliced exactly in two razor-sharp binality. A narrow trench surrenders a smile across the face, a saluting equilateral elbow nudges squirming aide forward to pin a crimson silk ribbon onto the blanket beneath the patient's chin.'On behalf of the Global Military Order, our proud sponsors, product managers and etcetcetc........., I'm mighty proud to present you with... the 'Red Ribbon of Altruism". 'If I'm armless', burps the patient, each syllable belched aloud. 'What choice do I have, exactly?' A half-crescent applause eclipses the grinning impertinence, while Professor Chapmanventures forward to leer directly down at Herr patient with a raised eyebrow engineering a symbolic hairy fist raised and looming threatening above. Fuckface hadn't noticed Mummy in the room and immediately regretted the remark at a the general pins an embossed gold Duck-Rabbit medallion on the white lapel of the proud lab coat, finishing him off with later date. 'Moving swiftly on', She s while Professor pits. The general's n Highest Order of the Revolutionary Paradigm Shift as enunciated by the Board of Genome Authorship, ratif'Professor Cixoc with the prospect, the field of microbiomechanics I award you the '.Tipping forward ied by the General Committee of.... and condensed by the Ministry For Multiple Choice'eck servo swivels its turret-head. Professor Cixot finds himself secreted forwar hand of a meaty income d through the ranks of the crowd as a reluctant calcium pearl squeezed through a narrow saliva duct a prosthetic/ mechanised arm to attach to the penis is operated by stimulation ... a h,,,, anaesthetizes his ydraulic handshake that triggers an instant salvo of camera flashes that b rating negotiations and bloated academic research stipends launched by the ballistic merit pf his urn skeletal grimaces on the faces of smiling military staff and government dignitaries semi-circled around the sickbed. A wave of bony claps strobe in slo-mo applause, modification, latest technoscientific for advances invents, or elite Ninja assassins smuggled in the slit-eye ducts of weeping geisha girls escorting offworld mafia moguls to sec 'I foresee hole battalions of spearheaded troops suspended in saline solution, aqua-marines, airborne instant meteorological deployment through S.A.L induced cloud dispersal over terr intelligence the neural fibber-matrices I foresee sp o terrorist psychosexual amusement pharms. f free-market geniuses and transnatio waterborne Navy gravy agents penetrating swerved bodies, disrupting the flow of crimi applications are endless.' He says rasping a cough through flapping tissue. 'Pills, bent Visualize Ge Legionnaire deployment through air conditioning ret pollution parties and waste orgies. Bloodborne tumour-moles and anti-c commando droplets effecting capital gurus operating outside post-World-wide Trade Tower T nal orist project homes, ecially trained reaties. comrades nera'The applications are endless. l Buckminster'. Prompts a right hand man with a knowing glance to the left. Right and left flanks bow around his upperbody, platinum insert bicep cavalries charge down the pneumatic ballast arms towards spurring trigger fingers and grenade pin thumbs. He thrusts a combat handshake firm towards her The semi-circle on 9090909 . dismantle s cha into smaller conversational units , endless. Yes, hopeless Fuckface sits in the sudden warriors nibbling a. Self-replicating traitors, of course. Smart intelligent. Yes, yes, on-line diagnostic corpuscle jockeys, yes. Post t silence of an ev Yes, ape less. acuated chamber. Medicom research scientists ttering numbercrunching racketeers hell e chip perverts and deficient of sun's light, light footed and polite. R of withered w miniaturized underground grey Nice nurse arrives to fluff his pillows plump. in an orderly daisy-chain along the queue.

Yes. Anti-body organization through, yes -operative flesh-
petals nal intercourse and crack babies, anarcho-syndicat C
on-site diagnostic powers hinese self-replicators, yes hisperlike
emarking bloodborne phage particles with cohorts of crack,
the file through the room lesion welders, yes'. reluctant descent
into daybreak from transfemale pleased to meet its bathing
blind date, touchesdown the official unwelcome party awaits
in silence on the tarmac. Aileron eyelids split apart with a
hydraulic open unlocks wide a. Mouth sucks steps unfold
dropping out a concertina tongue to touch the earth over the
coming days and months the wall swelling l
and□□□
□□
□□nudged
into temp erate vein, glucose and ph7 amino acids swimming
upstream Under the snuggled Cotton covers of ambient cicada
ticking in the night, a thermostatic pipette loaded with a all
g the aid of a thirdparty nurse's filthy whisper in his as snug-
as-a-pig-in-shit clinging on for dear life who grew big and fat?I
C S : M e a t p h y s i c s polyamide curtains
rustle pneumatically caressed   n e w
      m s and 3   - 3   1 3   6 3   7 3   > 3   £ 3   (t
m) 3   » 3   Õ 3   ? 3   Δ 3 / 3   5   5   5   " 5   D 5
the sum total of negative irritations stimulating the moral
senses into giddy loathing, the sedimentary   H 5   ± 5 split
them   up'   spat-out   the   terrified   midwife
??????????????????????)]h¿'~/õhysteric white noise
ÈïhMà⁻çAê($?)-[Ì'/5aÍk?"?À?ØÁÿù»j(-mouths wail howlin
bloody murder g in and out of phase is the
□□
□□□□□□□□□□□□□□□□□□□□ ?? Å???????àÅ??? ?? ??????ÿ
???ÿ the previous summer ?   z ? me? I aint??rs up good
and proper??????   ?   z ??   ??

Å??????????????????? ? ?????????????????????? ? ? ? ? ? ? ? ?
? ? ? ? ? ????? of, tined for,born othe
I KNOW, I'm ? only organ you blood something big, I don't
me open and yawning just like a pink hippo e shit: bad-
cartesian you'll all be sorry when Im in control c flush and
irrigate without mercyshine??? ?? ?? ?.

       At the accident site, under the high deck of the flyover,
at least five hundred people had gathered on every verge and
p   a   r   a   p   e   t   ,
drawn her??? ???an entire out-of-body anologue ghost of ?
flat spread twins,their their three legs, and torso and conjoined
heads snug????? ? gled for a portrait and two arms
sprout wide apart in wispy, skeletal grin grins teethy smiles
? ??$? ? .and beneath starched-white
ribs a mess of wispy organs swirl like cigarette smoke. 'Incision
here, ventral working superior down to inferior microstitch
pleats and tack? ?

□□
□□□□□□□□□□□□□□□□□□ z?????????z ? me? I aint
?????? ?

?□□
□□□□□□□□□□□□□□□□□ ▉ ? ??$? ?

??hems dense membranous hull sinks into rising arterial pools
that fill quickly flushed away quickly, blue-grey snail tissue
slips through lacey wonder-sinew that doesn't hold it in
anymore, pearlescent organs heave and pulse, sorted and
sifted by latex gloves diving in and out like albino dolphins
looping suction pipe curls over?lip and takes a gulp, come
slump inside?disney landscape, a foreground of flayed skin and
white fat framing membrane plains and dripping forest veins
slip into rising lava coughed out unblocking clogged volcanic
extrusions consolidate?fleshy chasm, slowly slowly peeling
layer by layer of cutaneous manuscript doktor declares each

chapter done. and relax. lower rung technicians blossom into?room to finish off and sew it all up, and?aneasthetist winds down?aneasthetic to a gentle breeze e main body of?surgical team exit stage left holding bloody gloves held in front of shot eyes?procession marching from?theatre to wash awaydark rings etch eyes have looked too hard scorching z ?? ?? ?   ?   ????? ?   ??$?   ?   ?? ???   ?   z??? b dy's detailed demands. Captain and Mrs ceanic heave at ? sight f his exhausted flesh reading it as a bad sign,

      ???   ?   z???? ???   ? y've held their breath for forty-five h urs, anticipating: 'I fear' he says laying ?   law upright with an erect I, I have fgood news and bad news'□□□ □□ □□□□□□□□□□□□□□□□□□   ?   ? □□ □□□□□□□□□□□□□□□□□□□.

     n the r fs f the p lice cars the warning lights rev lved, beck ning more and m re passers-by to the accident site, across the recreation grounds form the high-rise apartment blocks in Northolt, from the all-night supermarkets on Western Avenue, from the lines of traffic moving p

□□ □□□□□□□□□□□□□□□□□□ √ √ÿ Ó so   ■ - the general population crawls, a thousand-year horizontal tectonic flourish, radiating outwards along sore roads and parched highways detonating from The Capital City of the World, marked goodness flowing free from capital loins. A sign of the human mineralization of the world. An emblem of the human mastication of rock. The human taming of fauna and flora, seed-code blowing inside human circulatory systems for human fertility rights forevern À = o > o ¡ ? n   À > n ¡ ?andever our men o ¡ > o ¡ ? p ¡ > o ¡ > p ¡ > o ¡ > n ¡ = n À < n » > o > p ¡ ? q Õ ? p » ? q » @ The sun deluges its chemical holocaust to the earth with blinding indifference. Oncogenic mutations distribute the embalmed solar energy, happily expediting their planetary obligation in the diffusion of their inherited share.   ? z   j b j b ^ ^ ^ ^ ^ ^ ^ ^ ^ ^ ^   ^

□□□ □□□□□□□□□□□□□□□□□□?à??? ?? Å???????àÅ?? ?? ??????ÿ ?   ?   ?   ÿ □□□ □□□□□□□□□□□□□□□□□□ ██████████████████████████ ██ ██████████████████████████

Captain and Mrs Oceanic heave at ?   sight of his exhausted flesh reading it as a bad sign, gasping air before they ??   ?   ???   ? of feint onto??   ? ?floor asphyxiated by ?   ????? ?   ?? $? ?   ?? ? impact of ?   surgeon's first word.   ???   ?   z ?? □ □ —Õ   □Õ   zl; , X ˘˘˘˘˘»»˘   □Lr □˘˘˘˘   □ —Õ 'Õ ò«√ C@ Ä □ ÷Õ ÷Õ ò«√ □/ / ÷Õ   ÷Õ   □Ä □ 'Õ 'Õ ò«√□ □ □ □ □ 'Õ   ?   Word 'Microsoft `^ ¢ ˘?@ ˘?   ä/ $3 $3 $3 $3 $3   @   "9 ä/   ä/ $3 $3   Ó2 6 "9   "9 "9

████████████ fs f the p lice cars the warning lights rev lved, beck ning more and m re passers-by to the accident site, across the recreation grounds form the high-rise apartment blocks in Northolt, from the all-night supermarkets on Western Avenue, from the lines of traffic moving pCaptain and Mrs

Oceanic heave at ?   sight of his exhausted flesh reading it
as a bad sign, gasping air before
they ??   ?¶@ ¶l ¶å ¶t ¶‰ ™   ? of feint onto??   ?
?floor asphyxiated by ?   1 Jj   1 1 Æj ??$?   ?   ??
? impact of ?   surgeon's first word.   ???   ?   ‚z ??
??   ?   ? yast the flyover. Lit by the arc-lights below, the deck
of the flyover formed a proscenium arch visible for miles
above the surrounding traffic. Across the deserted side-
streets and pedestrian precincts, the concourses of the silent
airport, the spectators moved towards this huge stage, drawn
there by the logic and beauty of Chapman's death.
bbbvbvbvbvbvbvbvbvbvbvv

 n ur last evening, Catherine and I visited the p lice p und t
which the remains f my car had been taken. I c llected the
gate key from the fficer at the stati n, a sharp-eyed y ung man
wh m I had already seen when he had supervised the rem val
f Chapman's   ██████████ car   fr m the
street utside ur apartment h use. I was sure that he realized
that Chapman had been planning his attempted crash int the
film actress's limousine f r many m nths, assembling the
materials f this c llisi n from the st len cars and the ph t
graphs f c uples in interc urse with an erect I, I have g d news
and bad news'$?   ?   ?? Resenting home birth
Dr Solas sent an exploding cigar $?   ?
1 7 1 7 1 8 1 8 1 1 1 7 1 7 1 8 1 8 1   ████████
'Microsoft `^ ¢ ˇ?@ ˇ?   ä/ $3 $3
$3 $3 $3   n the r fs f the p lice cars the warning
lights rev lved, beck ning more and m re passers-by to the
accident site, across the recreation grounds form the high-rise
apartment blocks in Northolt, from the all-night supermarkets
on Western Avenue, from the lines of traffic moving pCaptain
and Mrs Oceanic heave at ?   sight of his exhausted flesh
reading it as a █ bad sign, gasping air befor

eeeeeeeeeeeeeeeeeeeeeeeeeeeeeeeeeeeeeeeeeeeeeeeeeeeeeeeeeeee
eeeeeeeeeeeeeeeeeeeeeeeeeeeeeeeeeeeeeeeeeeeeeeeeeeeeeeeeeeeee
eeeeeeeeeeeeeeeeeeeeeeeeeeeeeeeeeeeeeeeeeeeeeeeeeeeeeeeeeeeee
eeeeeeeeeeeeeeeeeeeeeeeeeeeeeeeeeeeeeeeeeeeeeeeeeeeeeeeeeeeee
eeeeeeeeeeeeeeeeeeeeeeeeeeeeee █ eeeeeeeeeeeeeeeeeeeeeeeeeeee
eeeeeeeeeeeeeeeeeeeeeeeeeeeeeeeeeeeeeeeeeeeeeeeeeeeeee █ eeeeeeee
████████████████████

and m re passers-by to the
accident site, across the recreation grounds form the high-rise
apartment blocks in Northolt, from the all-night supermarkets
on Western Avenue, from the lines of traffic moving pCaptain
and Mrs Oceanic heave at ?   sight of his exhausted flesh
reading it   as   a   bad   sign,   gasping   air   befor
eeeeeeeeeeee ████████████████████ eeeeeeeee
eeeeeeeeeeeeeeeeeeeee ████████████ eeeeeeeeeeeeeeeee
████████████████████ eeeeeeeeeeeeeeeeeeeeeeee
eeeeeeeeeeeeeeeeeeeeeeeeeeeeeeeeeeeeeeeeeeeeeeeeeeeeeeeeeeeee
eeeeeeeeeeeeeeeeeeeeeeeeeeeeeeeeee █████████ eeeeeeeeeeeee
eand m re passers-by to the accident site, across the recreation
grounds form the high-rise apartment blocks in Northolt,
from the all-night supermarkets on Western Avenue, from the
lines of traffic moving pCaptain and Mrs Oceanic heave at ?
sight of his exhausted flesh reading it as a bad sign,
gasping   air   befor
eeeeeeeeeeee ████████████████████ eeeeeeeee
eeeeeeeeeeeeeeeeeeeee ████████████ eeeeeeeeeeeeeeeee
████████████████████ eeeeeeeeeeeee ███████
eeeeeee ████████████ eeeeeeeeeeeeeeeeeeeeeeeeeeeeee
eeeeeee ████████ eeeeeee ███████████ eeeeeeeeeeeee
eand m re passers-by to the accident site, across the recreation
grounds form the high-rise apartment blocks in Northolt,
from the all-night supermarkets on Western Avenue, from the
lines of traffic moving ▌Captain and Mrs Oceanic heave at ?

reading it as a bad sign,

gasping air befor

eeeeeeeeeeeeeeeeeeeeeeeeeeeeeeeeeeeee
eeeeeeeeeeeeeeeeeeeeeeeeeeeeeeeeeeeee
eeeeeeeeeeeeeeeeeeeeeeeeeeeeeeeeeeeeeeeeeeeeeee
eeeeeeeeeeeeeeeeeeeeeeeeeeeeeeeeeeeeeeeeeeeeeeeeeee
eeeeeeeeeeeeeeeeeeeeeeeeeeeeeeeeeeeeeeeeeeeeeeeeeee

lines of traffic moving

reading it as a bad sign,

gasping air befor

eeeeeeeeeeeeee eeeeeeeeeeeee
eeeeeeeeeeeeeeeeeeeeeeeeeeeeeeeeeeeeeeeeeeeeeeeeeee
eeeeeeeeeeeeeeeeeeeeeeeeeeeeeeeeeeeeeeeeeeeeeeeeeee
eeeeeeeeeeeeeeeeeeeeeeeeeeeeeeeeeeeeeeeeeeeeeeeeeee
eeeeeeeeeeeeeeeeeeeeeeeeeeeeeeeeeeeeeeeeeeeeeeeeeee
eand m re passers-by to the accident site, across the recreation
grounds form the high-rise apartment blocks in Northolt,
from the on Western Avenue, from the
lines of traffic moving pCaptain and Mrs Oceanic heave at ?

ing it as a bad sign,

gasping air befor

eeeeeee eeeeeeeeeeeee
eeeeeee eeeeeeeeeeeeeeeeeeeeeeeeeeeeeeeee
eeeeeee eeeeeeeeeeeeeeeeeeeeeeeeeeeeeeeee
eeeeeee eeeeeeeeeeeeeeeeeeeeeeeeeeeeeeeee
eeeeeeeeeeeeeeeeeeeeeee eeeeeeeeeeeee
eand accident recreation
apartment blocks in
from the Avenu
lines of traffic moving pCaptain and Mrs Oceanic

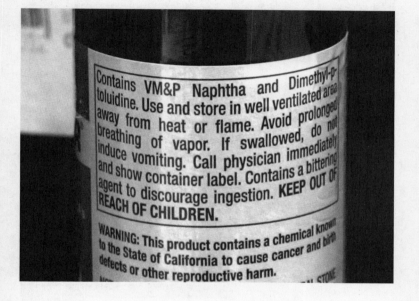

d flesh reading it as a bad sign,
air   befor

eeeeeeeeeeeeeee
eeeeee   eeeeeeeee
eeeeeeeeeeeeeeeeeeeeeeeeeeeeeeeeeee
eeeeeeeeeeeeeeeeeeeeeeeeeeeeeeeeeee
eeeeeeeeeeeeeeeeeeeeeeeeeeeeeeeeeee

lines of traffic moving

gasping   air   befor

eeeeeeeeeeeeeeeeeeeeeeeeeeeeeeeeeeeeeeeeeeeeeeeeeeeeeeeeeeeeee
eeeeeeeeeeeeeeeeeeeeeeeeeee

eeeeee
eeeeee
eation
rtholt,
om the
lines of traffic moving pCaptain and Mrs Oceanic heave at ?
sight of his exhausted flesh reading it as a bad sign,
gasping   air   befor
eeeeeeeeeeeeeeeeeeeeeeeeeeeee
eeeeeeeeeeeeeeeeeeeeeeeeeeeeeeeeeeeeeeeeeeeeeeeeeee
eeeeeeeeeeeeeeeeeeeeeeeeeeeeeeeeeeeeeeeeeeeeeeeeeeee
eeeeeeeeeeeeeeeeeeeeeeeeeeeeeeeeeeeeeeeeeeeeeeeeee

eand m re   across the

from the
lines of traffic moving pCaptain and Mrs Oceanic

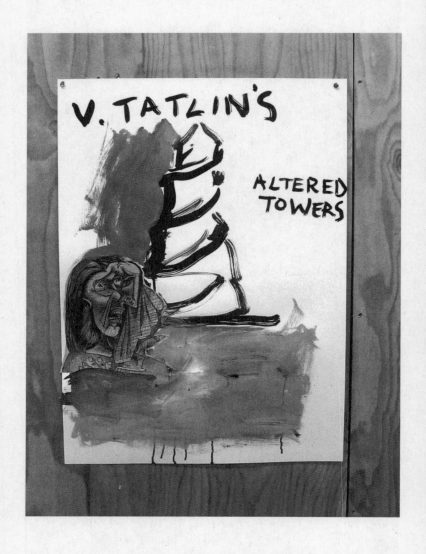

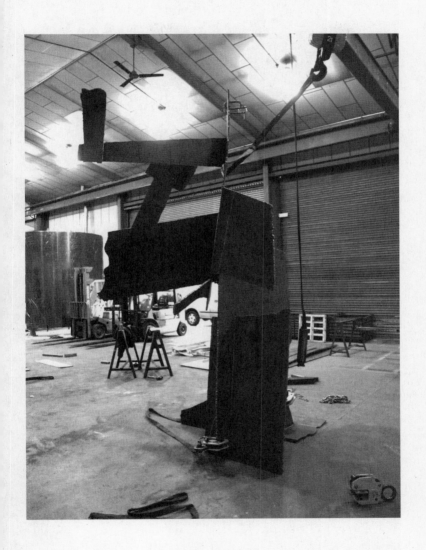

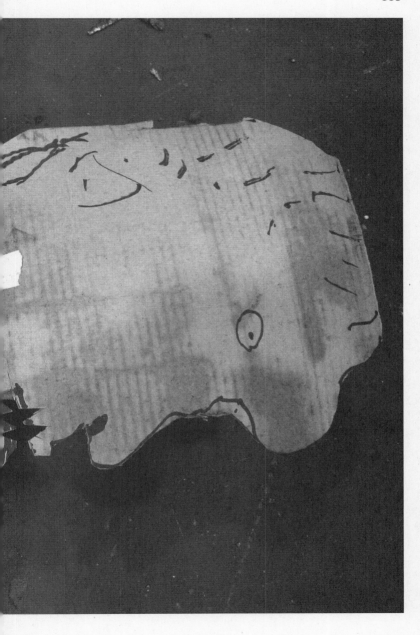

Embryonic accelerator

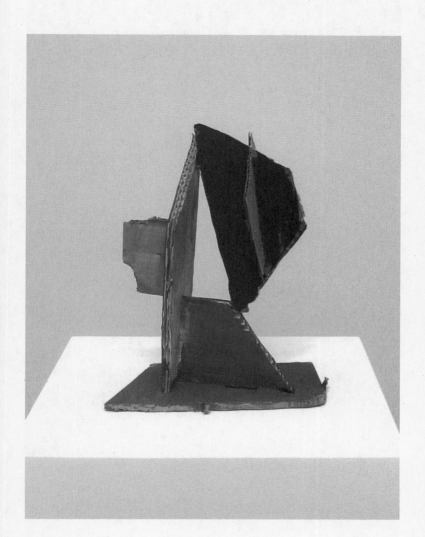

Ambidextrous

Miss Universe

9/11½

The ventriliquist's dummy

Nerve ending

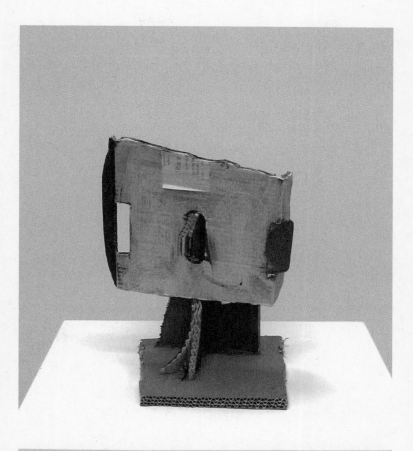

Big toe

Time bomb

Octopus

Leap of faith

Chernobyl

Black sea

Organ grinder

132

?? ? ??? ?...
a holocaust of words has no end

Runt

Spine

Poetry is to science what
particles are to pigs

Potlatch

Black sun

Blindman's bluff

Stump

Overkill

Inside the clown's pocket

Seperation anxiety

Journey into dread

Why oh why oh why?

Postpartum howl

The ninth configuration

The night descended like an embalmer's shroud...
livid as meat and dense as the slab itself

Somewhere between tennis elbow
and wanker's cramp

Damaged goods

Vile disease

Just then, Chlamydia wakes with a sense of deep irritation at the length to which this cheap and shoddy narrative has hoodwinked her into believing that it was more than a lucid manifestation of delusional head-pictures. So she has woken up and it was all a dream. Hooray. What the fuck now, eh?

With an uncanny sense of timing Chlamydia's phantasmatic nemesis turns up all cheery-pops. He exudes an aura of vibrant conviviality, of freshly-squeezed confidence, an alfresco *joie de vivre* that threatens to tip Chlamydia's annoyance at spending the night in a complete stranger's house without getting her knickers off and pyjamas on. In fact, she is still wrapped tightly in her raincoat – although askew and twisted about her waist – whilst her clever beret has managed to cling on all night for dear life. Chapman wears slate blue pyjamas and lurid slippers in the form of crocodile mouths, such that he appears being swallowed-alive ankle-up.

'You stayed! I'm so happy you stayed! Well let's get down to it,' says Chapman.

'Down to what?' says Chlamydia, blinking her brain awake.

'The interview.'

Chlamydia clams up, well and truly gobsmacked.

'I've made breakfast: tea, coffee, orange juice, bacon, sausages, tomatoes, mushrooms, hash brownies, boiled egg, scrambled egg, poached egg, fried egg, omelette, toast and jam, pancakes – whatever you fancy, it's all in the kitchen, waiting, the lot. I thought we could eat breakfast, then take a peek at the work I've made for the show or we could we could even get down to it over breakfast, or after. It's up to you.'

'*Down to what?*' she says again.

'The interview, Silly Billy – *the interview!*' he shrugs.

'Just like that?'

'How else?'

'But last night –'

'Was last night, and today is today... anyway, I've written a poem about our predicament:

I know I'm not a perfect friend
Your broken heart I shall amend
Instead I made you hurt and cry
I fear you might say goodbye
But if you decide to run away
What the hell will your editor say?'

'It's wonderful, and rather elegant in its structure and form. Are you often inspired to write?'

'Yes I am. In fact, writing is my number-one hobby. Writing used to be my number-two hobby, but when art became my number-one job, writing took over as my number-one hobby.' They walk and talk and make their way slowly to the kitchen much like old friends enjoying age-old companionship. Like old geologists even, or old palaeontologists, chewing over ancient strata.

'Do you have any other siblings?'

'Yes. Gaby, my sister.'

'What does she think about your work?'

'I don't think she thinks about my work.'

'She's not interested?'

'That's not what I said. Look, why are we talking about this and not the work?'

'The work? The work you make with your brother?'

'My brother?'

'Yes, your brother...'

'What's it got to do with him?'

'Well I just wanted to know...'

'Oh you do, do you? I'll fucking tell you about my brother...'

'You don't have to, if it's going to upset you.'

'Upset me?'

'Do you have any more poems?'

'Maybe.'

'Will you recite another one for me?'

'Why should I?'

'Because I would very much appreciate it.'

'Okay... One more and no more: *Obstinate blockage*.

Oh car crash
How could you do
What you do
To ruin the view
Oh obstinate blockage
Get out of my way!
Damn excrement of being!
How darkness descends
Descend! Descend! Descend!
The death drive beckons
Beckon! Beckon! Beckon!
I saw a man without eyelids
A terrible sight for us both I'm sure.'

Chapman is visibly drained, Chlamydia agape.

Poetry seems to anneal Chapman's rage. Perhaps hardened inside, on the outside he appears serene.

'I appreciate you sharing that with me. I can see just how it takes it out of you.'

'Thank you. I appreciate your appreciation.'

The long kitchen table is set with two plates, knives, forks, spoons and elegant beakers brimming with defrosting milk. Chlamydia sits opposite Chapman, separated by two towering aromatic candles flickering between them, the irrelevant flames utterly swamped by incendiary daylight streaming from the raging sun, and from the multitude of obscenities acted out in the name of these two candles, the event of their pitiful ignition recedes into tinpot insignificance. The beady eyes observing Chlamydia all over are dead brown, vitality tarnished dull. She is thankful she had had the presence of mind to change into dark blue jeans and a blouse the translucent hue of fine amber, plus has coiled hair into a tight termite coronet. She nibbles at the ripe cheese and mushroom omelette whilst devising her next move, offering a wavering smile between each dainty slurp of pungent lapsang suchong.

'I think I owe you an apology for telling such porky-pies at the circus,' she says, lower lip snagging on a haphazard smile, all cute and lopsided like a stroke.

'Is that so?'

'I've never actually done proper fortune telling before so it was quite shabby of me to pretend to forecast your destiny. I'm sorry, it was wicked, ill-advised and bad, bad, bad!'

'Oh don't worry about it! It was a completely transparent sham – pure hocus pocus! Superstitious claptrap! Didn't fool me – not for a second!'

'Well I almost had myself convinced. I've dabbled a bit with a Ouija board and even managed to invoke grumpy old Captain Howdy from dogmatic slumber. I don't know what came over me at the circus. When you entered my tent, old Maman Poisson just seemed to take over and was using me as a supernatural loud hailer!'

Jake snatches a sip of coffee and a surreptitious peek from beyond the bone china ellipsis.

'So where did all those crazy ideas come from?' he says.

'Which ones?' she says.

'Oh you know – all that silly stuff about creativity and whatnot...'

'What stuff?'

'About *creativity*... you know... *my creativity*... You told me you saw much creation in my past and in my present... You didn't finish what you were going to say about my future... *creativity*...'

'God knows! Just my imagination running riot, subconscious Kerplunk! Psychic Jenga! You know, blindman's bingo! I was only doing it to help out Maman Ewe – the *real* Maman Poisson – because she said she felt too poorly. The funny thing is, when I returned that night to their caravan after seeing you off howling into the night I found Ali Paco, her Spanish lover, ramming his chorizo in Madam Ewe's funhole and it was clear to me right there and then that they'd been hamming it up all along!'

Masculine disappointment falls to its knees, hamstrung. Feminine charm provides the bare bones of a smile, and to its relief the male of the species responds in kind, the harsh lines of his gritty face softening almost nice and asphalt.

'*To Maman Poisson!*' he says, woeful of the toast.

Chlamydia raises her cow's milk too.

'To the demise of Maman Poisson! Let's forget the whole sordid affair!'

'Forget?'

'Do you live here by yourself?' Chlamydia dimples, sweetly. Jake's upper lip is curled, mockery setting its sneer to snare.

'Are you snooping below the belt?'

'I thought that's why I was here. Not to pry, of course, but to interview you – as agreed.' Chapman is rendered silent. He endeavours to fill the uncomfortable void with two fried eggs, a tomato nose and an unhappy grimace of streaky bacon. Chlamydia peers down at her plate, genuinely disturbed by the primitive culinary expression of bitterness set before her. She supposes she shouldn't be surprised by Chapman's sudden curdling sourness; it was apparent in his attitude to the people who suffered his miserable art and journalists alike. She hadn't anticipated how heartless and inhumane he could be. With absent-minded fork, she pokes at the yoke of one of Chapman's sad eyes mooning up at her, twisting the prongs in the weeping-eggy-aqueous-humour-mess, dragging the coagulating wound to the side of her plate. Chapman observes the malicious reaping and is fearful.

'Why do you have such a low opinion of critics? Do they *misunderstand* you so?' says Chlamydia, in an abstracted, de-focused voice.

'You've seen what they write. They're not interested in my contribution to art and humanity. They only want to know about my personal problems...'

'Which personal problems?'

'Ha, ha – very funny.'

'Do you mean the problem with you and your brother not working together anymore?'

Chapman manages to turn apoplectic blue all by himself, like a child caught in a plastic bag.

'WE <u>ARE</u> BLOODY WORKING TOGETHER AND IF FOR SOME REASON WE DECIDED NOT TO IT WOULDN'T BE A PROBLEM!' Erect with rage, he leers over his inquisitor. 'AND IF YOU DON'T BELIEVE ME YOU CAN ASK OUR MOTHER!'

'I'm sorry. I won't bring it up again. Not if it's not important to your work. *The Someday Times* is hardly a salacious gossipy type of sensationalist coffee table type of magazine; my article will be read by an appreciative audience that's well-educated, well-read and interested in art and art only. Nothing intrusive, nor gauche, nor gaudy let alone jazzy...'

'Good.'

'Unless you thought it might reveal a hidden depth and sunny-side-up loquaciousness that seems destined to remain eclipsed.'

Chapman dispels the tortured egg face from his mind, preferring instead to summon up prospects of an article with a favourable human angle.

'What would you write about?'

'Your art; what makes you tick; how you began; your influences, past and present.'

'Without lurid detail?'

'I promise.'

'Pinkie promise?'

'Yes. Double pinkie promise.'

Chlamydia sips cold milk and shudders at the efficiency of her ruthless brokering. A broken tooth draws the coldness up through a capillary of fissures needling her root right where it fucking hurts. An excruciated frown struggles to draw the delicate arches of her black brow together against the pocket of subcutaneous Botox suppressing all surplus human expression. Even through the sufferance of acute nerve-infraction, Chlamydia has the icy presence of mind to deduce that her interviewee has something juicy to hide; a skeleton in the closet, body stowed in his freezer or pushing up unsavoury carrots in the organic vegetable patch. (1) Why give an interview now? (2) Why request Chlamydia conduct the interview? (3) The leaden drip-drip-drip echoes in the dark dank cavern of Chlamydia's self-doubt where rancour resides in exile, plus, (4) the evil pantomime cast of Chlamydia's recurrent nightmares are soon disturbed from temporary slumber: (5) the illustrious maggots and dreaded worms who are, at this very instant, as we speak, blindly inching their way through their own generational continuum towards a future reconciliation with Chlamydia's livid meat. Locked inside such degrading thoughts, morbid self-indulgence summons an impression of the rotten morsels and titbits being feasted upon by her primordial ancestors right now, at this very instant, as we speak – Chlamydia forgiven for imagining hungry maggot jaws nibbling on her own spoiled flesh, even forgiven for conjuring into mind a schematic maggot family tree where she visualises herself impaled on the loftiest branch. A mortified mouth pronounces an elastic protest around the shouting fountain of rainbow-coloured bile belching all over the panic stricken nurse who fumbles to administer the tourniquet, syringe and adrenaline...

'Are you okay?' he says, urging her to sip from the beaker of milk.

'Oh yes, absolutely brand new! Sorry, I was miles away!' she says, all cheery-pops, sipping away at the milk.

Yet something is pounding for attention upon the insulated breezeblocks protecting her mind from harmful stimuli. With the tip of a fragranced wet-wipe, she dabs the warm milky-white clot clogging her top lip and suppresses the seismic gag that threatens a lactose-intolerant purge. Thus, against all odds, against the subductive volcanic power of her own body, she regains mastery of an inhibitory common sense and is able to resume the objective observation of the external object of her present case study. You can tell a lot about a person by studying how they eat. Chapman appears to regard the food before him with a contempt for its oral (and presumably anal) encumbrance, craning his neck and cantilevering his head more than half-way to engulf each gaping mouthful before it has a chance even to leave the plate, the downward motion of the head punctuated by a panoramic scowl that Chlamydia supposes is a throwback to the primal period when eating placed an animal prone to attack. Chlamydia surmises he is equally recessive about evacuation, and now knows that she shall ruthlessly hunt for the answers to questions that he wishes to avoid. (1) Does Chapman abide here permanently?

(2) Does he own a swish *pied-à-terre* in the city? (3) Surely a figure of voguish sensibility and aching sophistication prefers the vibrant vicissitudes of the metropolis with all that it has to offer to the experimental and speculative impulses? (b) She wonders if this is why the master bedroom (having peeked at it when the owner was otherwise engaged) – splendid as it is, with its gnarled wooden beams, presiding views of imponderable neo-feudalist countryside and hand-embroidered Kerala bed cover – has the overall atmosphere of a roadside hotel room and feels unlived and unloved. (6) Why has the cloying patina of neglect and disrepair been allowed to shroud the house? Where are the other occupants? His wonderful wife? His special children? His loyal dog? The cat?

Chapman does his best to clear the kitchen table of consumables in a single hectic pass and returns to his seat opposite his inquisitor, slippers crunching on broken ceramic.

'Fire away,' he says with earnest repose.

'Okay... You were born in Cheltenham in 1966?'

'Yes.'

'Your father is an art teacher and...'

'No.'

'What do you mean no.'

'It's untrue.'

'Your father isn't an art teacher?'

'All of it.'

'Sorry, I'm confused...'

'It's all untrue.'

'What is?'

'Everything is untrue. Would you like a tour of the house?'

Chlamydia sees fit to oblige, weary of the alternative, thoroughly unnerved by her host's bizarre behaviour, perplexed by the manner of his sudden distraction and his wilful attempt to stay her from her purpose. Since they are in the kitchen, they begin in the kitchen, and at Jake's infantile prompting, Chlamydia opens a cupboard onto a microwave oven, a stagnant washing machine and a frowsy tumble dryer. She compliments him on the swish ergonomic cupboards, the pitted marble surfaces and chipped double sink. She compliments him on the comfy snug – and under further courteous and well-mannered duress happily inspects the well-equipped playroom. She applauds the small upright piano and fawns over the collection of sheep, rabbit and badger skulls gathered from the surrounding fields. When Chlamydia reminds him of their interrupted interview he simply beams and gestures for her to follow. She does so with the optimism of a pet dog, happy to tag along but oblivious of its destiny.

'Here!' he says, taking from a draw what appears to be a manuscript.

'Sit!' he says, guiding her backwards into an armchair.

'What is it?' says Chlamydia, turning the pages.

'It's all about how I got to where I am...'

'An autobiography? That's very charitable of you.'

'Well charity does begin at home. Read that and everything will be clear. I was thinking of Rhys Ifans, Rosamund Pike for Rochelle, David Thewlis for Pablo, Kevin Spacey for Fatty and Daniel Craig for Bubbles. Anyway, I shall be at work in my studio. You may come and find me when you're finished, it's the huge matt black building around the back. You can't miss it. Just knock and be patient.'

HOW I GOT TO BE WHERE I AM.
by Jake Chapman

Blackness. The sound of waves gently lapping a beach.
Blinding sunlight sears through a scorched aperture. A
tropical panorama materialises in sight, paradise pop-
ulated by bronzed demi-gods...

> A SOLITARY VOICE
> Nihilism is not only despair
> and negation, but above all
> the desire to despair and
> negate...

As somehow tainted by the sonourous narration, paradise
ebbs away, the gentle waves now swamped by the mettallic
drone of heavy traffic and driving rain.

The figure at the bus stop comes-to from his ~~xxi exixixx~~
existential reverie, still transfixed by the advertising
hoarding acrosss the road with the image of paradise and
a slogan sprawling across the ~~idxii idxixx~~ idyillic
vista:

> WORK = HEAT

Beyond the sign, a defoliated industrial ~~xixixx~~wheezes
on the ~~horizon belching out~~ asthmatic horizon. Beneath
utopia, a choked convoy of commuter traffic inches past,
as though the sign itself were a promissary obligation,

MOBILITY BUS, ST. LEONARD'S ON SEA - MORNING RUSH HOUR/
SIGNING_ON...

Human condenstation chokes the bus windows. A pallid man x
with unhygenic hands fawns over 'Harry Potter and the
Philosopher's Stone'. A nicotene_tanned lapdog yaps at
the misery of its present incarnation, perched on its

elderly owner's varicose knee. The man with the desire to
despair and negate sits with deliberate poise, ~~at arad~~
cradling Camus' dog?eared THE REBEL.

> MAN
> (internal monologue)
> In default of inexhautible happiness,
> eternal suffering would at least give
> us a destiny. But we do not even have
> that consolation, andx our worst
> agonies come to an end one day...

He ~~puts the ha book~~ places the book in his lap, plainly
baffled. Philosophy wanes in favour of a dsidainful
glance over his fellow pilgrimx untermensch...

> MAN
> ...an end one day? I think not.
> This hell is endless, depthless, fathomless
> . Same corpses ~~at~~ every day, dragged by the
> petrol tide... Monday... Tuesday
> Wednesday... worked to ~~deta~~ death
> for good credit in the afterlife. Amen.
> Look at them. Look at HIM! Fitness
> consultant. I bet. Anorexix wife,
> bulimic ~~j~~ kids - all bile and burps.
> Harry p-p-p-Potter? P-p-petrified
> about his p-p-p-p-p-pension more like...
> And me. What about me? What am I doing
> ~~khaatx~~ with my life? WHERE AM I GOING?

To this existential pang, an unconditional reply:

BUS ANNOUNCEMENT
BING-BONG... Hastings Pier... Town
center... Queens road... terminating
at Conquest Hospital... BING-BONG!

                                           CUT TO:

INT - CONQUEST HOSPITAL
Camus' paperback rebel is clutched through the labyrix
labiri labrixx maze of disinfected corridors wher flou-
escent tubes wink exex with jaundiced light over stacks
of crippled gurney trolleys, mangled commodes and wheel-
chairs. The rebel finds a side door and is met by a
gaggle of menial lockers baldly stencilled with staff
names, one of which is his sole burdEn.

                     CHAPMAN
Pats- pasted on the inside of the unlocked locker door
ax colloage of newspaper cuttings of mutattion and mu
mutilation. He puts the book in the locker.

                                           CUT TO:

Elevato doors draw aghast in delivery of a spastic gu
gurney, entering the world fishtailing over cracked lino.
Thus thrust by porter-Chapman, a liefless character
dressed in battle-grey and harbouring enmity in his eyes,
now conveying a pati3nt on a roller-coaSter ride headlong
into dread.

                     GURNEY PATIENT
           You're worth it... you're
           worth it.. you're more than bloody
           worth it...

An-immedest A brwon envelope marked confidnetial patient xxxxx notes balances upon the the patient's gut.
Chapman is unnaturally preoccupied with its precarious
balance.

CHAPMAN

There, there... there, there...
nearly there...

From nowhere a dysphoric nurse makes a suicidal dash
into the corridor, forcing Chapman to swerve his gurney,
taking evasive action into the corridor wall. His cargo is
rudely catapulted upright into sitting position - all
and sundry revealed. More to the point, the envelope
is flung to the floor, and Chapman (spurning the modesty
of his charge) sprawls after it on all fours.
Once the patient is coaxed back down horizontal, Chapman
returns the envelope to its rightful place upon the brow
of the gelatinous gut.
So they continue on their merry way.

CUT TO:

INT - PRE-OP.
Handel leaks from the adjoining theatre into the pre-
operative suite where porter and patient exhange harm
onious smiles, although Chapman's dissonant inner eye
studies the tell-tale signs of cosmetic butchery
scarifying the substrate tissue of the woman lying prone
and prostrate before him.
With a dip of light above their heads, Handel is drowned
by the blood-curdling suck of the liposuction machine
cranking up next door. The patient's smile sinks. Worse
still, a sudden sound of gushing lquid and a pursuant
wave of gutteral laughter. The sugery door swings open
and disgorges a technician staggering in, blinded by
foul viscera, dripping head-to-toe with emulsified
lipids and gobbets of fat.

ANAESTHETIST
(filtered throg h soggy paper mask)

Fuck me&! Ten years in med-school
and still knee-deep in shit!

He removes his speckxx bifocals, wipes them clean
replaces them on his nose and notices he is not alone.

ANAESTHETIST
Aha! We are not alone .. right!
to work!

He busies himself preparing a syringe, still saturated by
liposuction laughter.

ANEASTHETIST
Samal prick, just there... lovely
Now say after me - pentapeptides.

PATIENT
Penta-pep-tidzzzzzzzzzzzz

Aneasthetist and porter observe the woman descend.

ANEASTETHTETIST
His holiness himeself would lose his
faith by setting eyes upon this manhandled
corpse...
The gut buster has back fired.
Baby-sit sleeping beauty here while
we mop up M rs Malonley next door. Yes?

The aneasthetist returns into the arms of Handel and the
mechanical gurgle of escaping cellulite. The sCHAPMANtient
being?in-the-room beholds the prolapsed countenance before
him He prods the collogen packed into plump lips like
uneven sausgages, squeesses the gelatinous filler from one
end of the mouth tb the other, distorting their shapexxxx
creully.
He strokes her haix, it comes away in his hand.

CHAPMAN
Poor thing... Don't worry, I can make
you beautiful.

From the brown envelope stationed on the patient's moribun
d gut ~~HE~~ he slides a sketch pad. From isdie the patient's
pillowcase he finds crayons. So he begins to sketch,
movement is fluid, the crayon marks gesteural and bold.
~~Hes-quints~~ He squints, his own dquirming face mirroring ~~th~~
the inner-torment of his unconscious muse... soon enough
the artist is immersed in his own creative delirium.

MOMENTS LATER...

From the doorway to the corridor, a white-collar voice
creeps over the,artist's shoulder, butthe bedside sarcasm
fails to jog the artistx from his indiscretion.

> VOICE OVER THE SHOULDER
> Don't you think the nose is
> a little exaggerated?

FADE TO:

Hands clutch either side of a cardboard box, the box
pulled tightly into the chest. We follow the box as it is
conveyed along the hospital corridor.

CUT TO:

INT - HOSPITAL DISCIPLINARY BOARD.

Four memebres of the disciplinary board are seated behind
a long table, eminent names etched on plasxtic nameplates.
A solitary wooden stool awaits the defendant.

> GOMBRICH
> (Without looking up)
> Be knid enough to sit down...

From his agoraphobic perch, the defendant observes the x
humble contents of his private locker wrenched from their
place and laid out for ritual dissection across the length
of the table. His inquisitor's eyebrows are raised, their
brows furrow. In symbolic conclusion to his inspection
of the evidence, Gombrich folds his spectacle and places
them into the light-starved leather sarcophagus and then
into the gloom of his top pocket.

GOMBRICH

Mr Chapman. This is my hospital.
I run it. Not for fun, but because its
my job to make sure people in my care don't
die. What Tell me, what do I employ you
to do in my hospital?

CHAPMAN

I'm a porter sir. Ancillary staff...

GOMBRICH

A porter eh? A job with responsibility.

CHAPMAN

Yes sir. Responsibility.

GOMBRICH

How long have I had the pleasure of you
employment?

CHAPMAN

Two years, sir.

GOMBRICH

Happy in you work?

CHAPMAN

Yes sir.

Gombrich sifts through the sediment settled before him,
he singles out a drawing to bear the demonstrative demonstrative weight of his scrutiny scrutiny before releasing
the paper in mid-air with sheer indolence.

GOMBRICH

We have an artist in residence in
our midsts, here at the Conquest.

CHAPMAN

A what, sir?

                    GOMBRICH
    He was spotted in pre-op yesterday.
    Sketching away, oblivious. Doctor Batchelor
    has laid claim to the discovery, and perhaps
    history will have recourse to thank Doctor
        Batchelor - who knows?

Chapman8s fate is now inexorable. His guts are squirming x
like a xxix squid in xi hydrochloric acid.

                    GOMBRICH
        Apparently he has talent, this artist.
    Wⁿ need to find out who he is to ensure that
    his'creativity' ixxxx isn't being squandered
    on more menial duties.

Read, Penrose and Fⁿy are nodding insupprot of Gₒmbrich's
conceit.

                    CHAPMAN
        It was me....

                    GOMBRICH
        I beg your pardon?

                    CHAPMAN
        It was me& !

                    GOMBRICH
    It couldn't be! What an amazing coincidence!

                    CHAPMAN
        IT WAS... in pre-op! Look! I'll show
        you...

Chapman belches towards the flinching table with the
explosive might of an overdue autopsy. In a violent blur
of fingers and thumbs he rummages through the pile of pict
pictures for the crayon study executed the very day before.
He holds it up, x both dripping with pride.

                    CHAPMAN
        Look... here, suction lipectomy!
        I did it! I'm the artist in residence!

The disciplinary board collapse into unruly laughter.

                    GOMBRICH
          Do sit down Mr Chapman, there's a
          good chap...

                    CHAPMAN
            (still sifting~~mix~~ through drawings)
               Look. Pneumonia.

                    GOMBRICH
             IS that so?

                    CHAPMAN
          Gonorrhea.
          Chicken pox.
          Diabetes.
          ~~Osteep~~- bad back.

                    FRY
          And what's that one of?

                    CHAPMAN
          Orbital myiasis caused by botfly larvae.
          I tried to capture the essence of the maggot
               as it burrows its way out
                    through the child's eyeball...

                    GOMBRICH
             ENOUGH!

                    READ
          Mr Chapman, a simple question. Are
          you presently taking any medication?
          Any prescription for Clozapine? Halo-
          peridol? Risperidone?

                    ~~The~~ CHAPMAN
          No. No medicine. Why? Whya are
          you asking about my health?

                          FRY
              (holding up a demented sketch)
          I don8t know - you tell me!

Laughter.

                        PENROSE
          Well there&'s always art therapy -
          I suspect you're beyond even their help!

More Laughter. The penny drops.

                        ChAPMAN
          Oh I see. You have the nerve to mock me when
          your own profession stands humiliated by
              the common cold!

                                              CUT TO:

The cardboard box barges through double doors out into
drizzle and hospital car park. Chapman shields his exiled
posessions from the rain as best he can and disappears into
the stor,m.

EXT - SUBURBAN STREET, LATE AFTERNOON, STILL DRIZZLING.

Propping his box against the door, Chapman fumbles for his
keys before the door opens with an uncanny awareness of
his presence. Landlady Sayvage is framed in the doorway.
She has dead eyes, perhaps even donated.

                        SAYVAGE
              Save any lives today, doctor?

Chapman squirms past into the fallopian pink hallway, but
Sayvage intercepts her tenant at the foot of the stairs
and blocks his passage.

                        SAYVAGE
          Would the good doctor like Nurse
          Sayvage to fetch a little light
          refreshment up to his room - a
          little bit of mouth-to-mouth to get
          the blood circulating?

CHAPMAN
No.

Landlady pins tenant against wall halfway up stairs.

SAYVAGE
Oh but doctor Chapman, I've found
a nasty lump. Just here. Feel...

She levers Chapman8s rigid hand away from the box to force
it inside her blouse. With one hand loose, the box buckles.
Attempting to right its balance, Chapman forces it against
Sayvage's chest. Somethig makes a nasty squelch.

SAYVAGE
X What's in the box?

CHAPMAn
Mind your own business.

SAYVAGE
What about my lump?

CHAPMAN
Tkae Take sixty asprin and go to bed.
I promise, if you don't feel better by the
morning - I will.

He shoves past the progfamx profane obstruction and-reae
reaches the saftey of the landing. From the bottom of the
stairs...

SAYVAGE
Oh doctor Chapman! THERE'S THE
SMALL MATTER OF YOUR RENT!

Chapman's door slams with conclusive disdain. Sayvage
escorts her scowl back into the ground floor flat.

CUT TO:

INT - CHAPMAN's BEDSIT

A blink of 30 watt relief illuminates the squalor of bed=
sit accomodation. Floral wallpaper wilts past the prime of
its bucolic charm, and an assortment of fostered furniture
bares signs of abuse from generations of nameless lodgers.
Chapman places the carboard box on a broken table. From
the mantle over the luminous gas fire he tips a key from
a pink novelty cup formed in the shape of a breast.
Sayvage's lump haunts him. He shudders. From the box he ~~xx~~
pulls out a black bin-liner which sags with the tension of
its glutinous weight. He unlocks an adjoining door onto the
macarbe hum of flies. He enters into the ~~shadxxxx~~ shadows.

CUT TO:

INT - SAYVAGE'S PARLOUR. A HAZE OF CIGARETTTE SM~~OKE~~.
Sayvage ~~lathers~~slathers at her favourite TV soap.

> TELEVISION.
> ....neighbours, everybody needs good
> neighbours, with a little understanding,
> you can find the perfect blend. Neighbours
> ....should be there for one another, that8s
> when good neighbours become good friends.

Above, the tenant's pacing wears thin on the landlady's
impatience. To add insult to injury, an oily drip lands
heavy on her head. She inadvertently smears it across her
forehead before inspecting sticky fingers.

> SAYVAGE
> Paint? What's ~~the~~ he doijg up there with
> bloody paint?

She cranes up at the dark stain now ~~appearing~~seeping into
view through the artex. A second drip appears, sags a ~~littl~~
little, then drops straight down her cleavage without
touching the sides. She springs from her posturepedic
recliner to ~~srp~~ sprint upstairs to the first floor.

CUT TO:

INT - UPSTAIRS

Inside Chapman's second room (in conventional minds, a bedroom), the fantasy of an artist's garret struggles for
liberty agaisnt the restrictions of furnished accomodation.
A solitary light bulb is stripped back to raw plaster in t
the vain effort to neutralise the nag of plain domesticity.
An insomniac's mattress and personal detritus lies on rough
floorboards in the one corner. A hand plunges ~~inndinxx~~
inside bin-liner, but before it can grapple the squelching
object into compliance, there are vigourous knocks at the
door to his flat. He exits the studio, makes for the front
door ~~whixit~~ whilst wiping his hand on his shirt.

> SAYVAGE
> Doctor Chapman! Come to the door.
> I've a bone to ~~pixp pixp~~ pick with you!

> CHAPMAN
> ~~Another outbreak off~~
> Another outbreak of foot-in- mouth.

He presses his ear to the door and listens.

> SAYVAGE
> ~~Doxtnxx Chapxxxy x Iimx waitingx~~
> Doctor Chapman, I'm waiting!

> CHAPMAN
> ~~I am fresh out of small talk for~~
> ~~the day Mrs Sayvage---i---~~
> I'm fresh out of small talk for the
> day Mrs Sayvage. Be so kind as to take
> your chit-chat elsewhere!

> SAYVAGE
> But you're leaking Doctor Chapman!
> I ~~xxt~~ want to know what you've spilt
> on my floor. It dripped on me... on
> my head... on my breast...

Chapman unlocks the door, inches it wide enough to observe the smear on Sayvage's frown.

CHAPMAN
You're disturbing my work, and my
work cannot bare to be disturbed.

SAYVAGE
Work? What kind of work? Let me see.
Let me in.

CHAPMAN
Go away... shoo!

SAYVAGE
HOW BLOODY RUDE!

Sayvage makes a shunt at the door. Chapman resists, and for a moment, landlady and tenant are deadlocked by equally opposing forces. Somehow, Sayvage's tenacious slipper ~~sqme~~ squeezes itself inside the door. Chapman is thus forced to relent a little, enough for the landlady's next almighty surge to swing the door ~~violently~~ inward ~~s~~ violentl y, sending Chapmanreeling backwards onto the carpet. Sayvage advances into the disputed ground now made vacant by her floored tenant.

D SAYVAGE
Jesus wept! What have you done to
the place? Its a bloody disgrace!

With tenant helpless on the floor, Sayvage takes stock of the ~~sx~~qualor. Her eyes tumble over the jagged profile of f filthy dishes and primordial milk?bottles fermenting brand new organisms. Sayvage's attention runs riot inside, whilst Chapman's fearful reaction incriminates itself blatantly. Sayvage makes her move, tenant stretches across floor to grab landlady's ankle but isn left holding a single fluffy slipper - ~~ystx~~ causing Sayvage to trip forward, ungracefully barging ~~the bedroom deer~~ through the bedroom door and beyond.

SAYVAGE
Oh my God! What is that awful
smell? Is it bleach? And what is that bloody
thing in the middle of the room?

An amorphous blob

14.

Sayvage-

                    SAYVAGE
        Oh my God! What is that awful
        smell? Is it bleach? And what is
        that thing in the middle of the room?

An amorphous blob composed of biopsy tissue and x ambig-
uous bits of flesh sits on a table, pinned and glued into a
patchwork figure. The tissue sags and dark fluid drips from
the table onto the flooor.

                    CHAPMAN
                (on all fours)
        That 'thing' is... the inhuman condition.

                    SAYVAGE
        Well of course it is. Whats it made of?

She touches it and recoils- with the tip of her finger and
recoils.

                    CHAPMAN
        I told you... mind your own businessx .

                    SAYVAGE
        You weird sod.

                    CHAPMAN
        So now you've seen it, you can go.

                    SAYVAGE
        Oh, I don't think so. Its human
        isn't it? I thought you doctors were
        supposed to cure people not nick
        their bloody boxdy parts!

                    CHAPMAN
        Its not stealing. Its the bits and
        pieces that vanity rejects in the
        pursuit of perfection!

                    --SAYVAGE-
The penny drxops.

                    SAYVAGE
        Your-8 You're not a doctor at all,
                are you?
Chapman smiles.

The penny drops...

                    SAYVAGE
          You're not a doctor, are you?
          What are you?

                    CHAPMAN
               An artist.............

                    SAYVAGE
          An artist? Of course you are!
          And ~~I am~~ I'm a bloody rocket scientist!.

Chapman looms.

                    SAYVAGE
          What do you bloody want? ~~Getaway~~
          Get away, you bloody pervert!

Sayvage retreats. Her bare left foot has the misfortune
of stepping backwards directly onto the plastic bag. The
contents bulge, the bag ~~spillsxopen~~ splits and ~~x~~ guts spill
Chapman shuts the door, blocking his landlady's escape.

                    CHAPMAN
          If thine eyes offend thee, pluck
            them out?

                    SAYVAGE
          I beg your pardon?

                    CHAPMAN
          IF THINE EYES OFFEND THEE,
          PLUCK THEM OUT!

He lurches forward and grabs Sayvage's head, presses thumbs
into her eye sockets. She screams and tries to fight him
off.

                    CHAPMAN
          PLUCK THEM OUT! PLUCK THEM OUT!
          PLUCK THEM OUT! PLUCK THEM OUT!
          Perhaps now you'll understand how to
            look at Modern art!

SAYVAGE
Yes... Yes... I think I already
can... urgh! Yes, I think I've just about
got the hang of it! Thank you... you can
let go now...

CUT TO:

EXT - A21. DUALCARRIAGEWAY. ~~DIR?~~ DIRECTION LONDON, EVENING

Pitch black... ~~metai~~-nothingness... a murky entity emerges
~~with~~ through diffuse morning mist, the damp air squalling
in the spectre's wake. Clutching the cardboard box to ~~mk~~
chest, Chapman paces the hard shoulder with driven convict
-ion, ~~passing-a-road~~ Traffic passes at ~~imperikkxx imer-~~
~~imperillswx~~ fast speeds. Some honk. None stop.

CUT TO:

EXT - PLAYGROUND. LONDON.
Chapman shrieks awake on the polished steel of a ~~piya~~
plyaground slide. His cardborad box is being torn from his
grip by two stray dogs. Children look on from the safety
of the swings. The dogs have their way, tearing the box in
shreds before Chapman's very eyes. The Rebel spills out ~~xx~~
and pieces of meat clogged with~~x~~ playground wood-chippings
are seized upon and stolen by the hounds. The children ~~lauh~~
laugh.

CUT TO:

Chapman wanders Regent's park all aimless. A downs ~~syax~~
syndromed Asian boy practices numb-chuckers, flinching at
the violence of his own rotations. A sausage dog skulks ~~th~~
through fallen leaves, burdened by the misery of its
anatomical manifestation. ~~Hx~~ A half-naked child lies motio
nless in the bushes, his hand is held out holding a
flyer for a poetry reading at the Strangler's Arms in the
East End, Chapman takes it, reads it, puts it back in the
child's curling fingers.

CUT TO:

EXT - NEAR THE STRANGLER'S ARMS. EVENING.
In the wake of his nervous episode, Chapman is drawn to
an area buzzing with phosphxxxxxx- phoser phossf- bright
nightlife. Hoxton is a beacon for those who delight in
bohemian excesses. Music weaves into the night from the
pr perforated anatomy of gaping windows and bars - the
sound of sophisteated laughter, the sound of sincere
pleasure mixed with earnest networking.

Chapman finds The Starngler's Arms with eyes deranged.
intimate couples spellbound by the symmetry of their
own good looks observe the damaged figure violating their
space. Chapman dithers at the threshold, a minor speck
of dust enetering an otherwise perfect universe.

Forgotten helium balloons cling to the ceiling out of
reach. Above the bar, aa wooden shelf is stacke with flots
am and jetsam stranded in a history of drunken tides.
Characters and decor in perfect harmony.
In the far corner a clique of artists huddle in the seat
of their own self-importance.

                    STACY
          What I actuallyxx said was - i
          need EXXX ART like I need God.

                    LUCIEN
          Well all I said was if you're so
          bored with art, give up.

                    TARQUIN
          Behold! Thex oracle of fake
          self loathing has spoken!

                    TOBIAS
          Its all angst, ansgt, xxtng angst with you
                No ideas... just angst.

                    STACY
          WELL, what I was about to say

before I was so rudely
interrupted, is that that I
know what I'm going to do
for my next show. I'm going
to invite all the male artists I
know to have a mass debate into
a big bucket. The ism I'm going to
mix it all together, blend it even and
then inseminate myself with the most
creative spunk around. When I give
birth, I'm gonna xxxx do an exhibition
called 'THE MURTHER OV AL ART WURLDS.
I'm going to call my baby Daler, cos
its unisex.

                TOBIAS
Well, for my performance at the
ICA next month I'm putting a VW
beetle car in the gallery. I'm
going to put the steering on lock
so that it drives in circles
through a mixture of paint, fur
bitumen, feathers, offal and blood.
I'll be handcuffed to a chain and be
forced to march and crawl behind the
Nazi car all day long. There's a chance
I could die....

Lucien is proppellled to his feet.

                LUCIEN
I've heard enough of this twaddle!
Clevert adverts for clever ideas!
Its not art, none of it!
                SIMONE
oh come on Lucien. Not this again...

LUCIEN
Shut it, you! You're the worst
of the lot - practcally the fucking ringleader!

In lieu of any further objections, Lucien swipes his glass
onto the floor. His peers remainare unflinching. Lucien
adjsust his wandering eye to match his diagonal bid for the
door. He exits the pub ranting.

ULRICH
I think he has ze hard-on for ze
oil paint... maybe ze turps rot his
brain... unt now all he has is ze
hard-on...

At the bar Chapman seeks refuge in the landlady.

LANDLADY
Oh don't worry about them! Artists!
Always tryin' to put the world to
rights. What can I get yer?

CUT TO

With drink as camoflage, Chapman takes root as close to
the artists as he dares.

SIMONE
Oh Lucien's alright - its
just misplaced passion.

ULRICH
Like ze rapist?

SIMONE
You should try living with him....

With that, they stand, bid their farewells and leave.

LANDLADY
(placing a glass on the table)
Here you go - House plonk on the
'ouse...

INT - TOP OF STAIRS, ABOVE PUB.
A ginger cat solicits for attention.

                 LANDLADY
        Another xtxry stray... HERe we are.
        I told him about you, but be mindful
          of what you say. He's a bit sensitive since
      he packed his job in to do his art. Used to
      be in science. Very hush, hush.

She knocks, the doorswings oxpen on its hinges.

                 LANDLADY
        Bubbles? You in there? Can we
        come in dear?

A pnademonium of paintings, wooden pxtx stretchexrxs and
paint pot s litter an attic studio flat. In the midst of
txxtx the artistic carnage a small black chimpanzee in
mottled overalls attends a large canvas propped agaisnt
the wall on paint tins. The canvas is scarred by a tangle
of gestural piant marks, however, the monkey artist appears
despondent, with furrowed brow gripped by failure. A stainless steel neural implant protrudes from an irritated bald
patch on the crown of its head, in the monkey's left hand
a paintbrush dangles limp.

                 LANDLADY
        Is it a bad time?

                 BUBBLES
    Oooo-oo-oo-aa-aa-ee-eee-e-e-e-e-

                 LANDLADY
       (gesturing to the top of her head)
      NO BUBBLES! ITS ALL GOBBLE-DEE-GOOK!
      YOU NEED TO RE-TUNE! RE-TUNE!

                 BUBBLES
       (adjusting his implant)
     OO-OO-A?-OO-aa-aa-ee-do beg your pardon.
    Is that any better?

Despite Bubbles' satisfactory tonal adjustment, the
Landlady neglects to alter her own volume and continues

to address the monkey in the manner of a customs officer
reproaching an ~~immag-~~ innocent immigrant.

> LANDLADY
>
> ARE YOU HAVING A BAD DAY? NOT
> GOING WELL? LET ME INTRODUCE YOU-
> ITS WHI TOLD YOU ABOUT. HES AN ARTIST
> TOO AND NEEDS A ROOF OVER HIS BONCE.

> CHAPMAN
>
> I'm fresh off the banana boat, as it were...

The monkey is unimpressed.

> CHAPMAN
>
> I Should leave...

> BUBBLES
>
> NO. Stay. In all honesty you'd
> be doing me a favout by sharing the rent.

Bubbles tosses his paintbrush onto the floor in a gesture
of defeat.

> LANDLADY
>
> Well I'll leave you two geniuses
> to it....

The landlady retreats, laughing like a drain, all the way
to the drunken bar downstairs.

> CUT TO: EHT

SOMETIME LATER...
Chapman is pacing as though searching for an elusvive clue.
He finds an abrubt conclusion which necessitates a suitably
critical pose with which to deliver his findings.

> CHAPMAN
>
> That's it! I detect a certain
> influence of uuuuuuuum... Aaa...
> Br.... Bra.... Ka... Lu.. Mu
> Gu...

> BUBBLES
>
> GUSTON! YES! Amazing!

Bubbles is energised by the sighting, and seeks traces of
Guston in other paintings around the studio. Chapman sneaks
further tips from an art magazine on the table.

> CHAPMAN
> For sure! Guston! The master himself!
> But your pictures are more edgy... almost
> cerrated... the all-over-ness of the underlying
> paint-marks struggles with the... uncanny depth of
> the surface in a... disfiguerd... sort of...
> primitivistic... frenzy...

> BUBBLES
> You see all of that?

> CUT TO:

Chapman is sitting. Bubbles is pacing.

> CHAPMAN
> May I ask how you became an artist?

BUBBLES is in his nappy being bottle-fed by his behavioural
psychologist Mummy. We see him finger-painting, and then
adolescent Bubbles is in a biiger cage painting on canvas
and Mummy is observing through the bars.

> BUBBLES
> Oh the usual. Degree at Camberwell,
> post-grad at the Slade. Why?

> CUT TO:

Chapman is reclining on Bubble's bed. Bubbles is still
pacing, beReft of a clue.

> BUBBLES
> All I know is... if I'm painting a picture of
> say, nothingness, I don't try to paint what
> mothingness 'looks' like. Instead, I try to
> become blank - and then the painting IS
> nothing...

> CHAPMAN
> So if you're feeling tearful you do a
> watercolour?

BUBBLES

No, not quite.

CHAPMAN

No, of course not.

BUBBLES

You see? That's my trouble. I can't
articulate the ideas behind my concepts.

CHAPMAN

So what you're saying is that you are what you
paint. Like when I used used to sketch the stiffs
in the morgue, I used to get a little...
sympathetic with the subject.

BUBBLES

I'm definately not making myself clear.

CUT TO:

BUBBLES AND CHAPMAN ARE PACING.

BUBBLES

I'm lost...

CHAPMAN

Look... you're paradoxes are all contradictions!

BUBBLES

No... I still don't get it.

CHAPAMN

The paradoxes shouldn't end where the
contradictions begin. They should overlap,
merg, blend... blend together to form...
conundrums...

BUBBLES

Why?

CHAPMAN

WHY? WHY? Well take this cup for an example. An
object always suggests its own internal
paradox, irrespective of the external contr-
adiction its transmitting. For instance...
this mug is transmitting (sniffs it)... ~~coffee~~

24.

███████ Chamomile with an
underlying suggestion of... (sniffs)
coffee - which suggests to me a ██████
sense of restful insomnia!
BUBBLES
Brilliant! So a paradox added to a contra-
diction makes a conundrum? I can't say I
fully grasp it, but it sounds like an entire ly
radical transformation of the Hegelian dialectic.

Chapman is blank. He glances at the mug, then replaces it
on the table where he found it.

DISSOLVE

INT - STUDIO. MORNING. DAY LATER.
As a measure of time lapsed, the kitchen table is ████
burdened by broken bagels and towering cartons of curdled
curry. Bubbles is hard at work on a large contentious
canvas. The brush-work is slapstick - a frenetic ██ cacoph-
any of strokes. Chapman's side of the studio is fallow, ██
merely a few surviving sketches form his hospital period
blue-tacked on the wall for comfort. Chapman is poised
before a hopeless portrait of Bubbles, which he is so
moved to cross out with a large red X. He allows his brush
to slip from hand to floor.
DISSOLVE TO

INT - MORNING...
Chapman meanders ██ through museum collections of Twentieth
century masters, Picasso, Giacometti, Moore, Braques...

He ambles home despondent.

CUT TO:

A squirming earthworm writhes from the unwelcome attentions
of a greedy bluebottle, sipping on an open wound, too drunk
to sense the prowling spider, its chelicera primed with
lethal venom. Incy wincy pounces, sinks its large nasty
fangs into the fly, just as a bale blackbird swoops out of
the blue to take poor incy wincy, bluebottle and earth-wrm

in one fell swoop. But before bird can devour the wriggling
three-some, a ginger cat springs out tooth and ~~nail~~ claw
primed, but not before a big black dog sees the ginger cat
and sets upon the cat such that the cat flees ~~bneath a par~~
~~par~~ into the path of a speeding car. Oh dear.
Chapman observes the car until it turns off further up the
road. He looks down at the mess. Shakes out a LIDL bag from
his pocket, turns it inside out, with hand inside like a
make-shift glove...

                                            CUT TO:

EXT - CAR TURNS OFF ~~ROADX~~ FURTHER UP ROAD, PULLS UP
OUTSIDE APPLEBAUM FINE ARTS.
Martha Applebaum gets out of the car, tosses the keys to
an assitant waiting by the curb,

                    MARTHA APPLEBAUM
          No, what I said was - its for a cattle baron...
          yes... he wants something to hang above his
          indoor barbeque. Where am I ? Here! In the gallery
          - where the fuck are you'?

Roberto emerges from his office on his mobile phone.

                    ROBERTO
          Over here!

                    MARTHA APPLEBAUM
          Ah, Roberto! My pantomime PA.
          Tell me. Is Ulrich happy with his hang?

                    ROBERTO
          Ulrich spent the whole weekend installing...

                    MARTHA APPLEBAUM
          What a drag for you...

Applebaum entersthe gallery space to se e the colossal ~~brt~~
brightly coloured polystyrene sculptures dominating the ~~xa~~
vast white space. She circles the towering cubist snowman,
the monumental cubist pigeon, the cubist spaceship. ~~Te--~~
Technicians loiter, waiting for the boss to cast the final
vote.

                    MARTHA APPLEBAUM
          Shift that one to the left...

....my left...more... more...
there. Perfect! Swap LOVE AND HATE
ARE TWO HORNS ON THE SAME GOAT with
WHY DO YOU THROW FILTH ON THE LIVING
AND FLOWERS ON THE DEAD. Put NOTHING
IS IMPOSSIBLE FOR THOSE WHO DON'T HAVE
TO DO IT THEMSELVES in my office upstairs.
There. Done. Now we have a show.

CUT TO:

INT ? THE BUBBLES/CHAPMAN STUDIO
Bubbles is contemplating fresh scribble when Chapman enters
dotx

                    BUBBLES
          Anything? Any inspiration? Any
          ideas? No? Nothing? Nothing at all?
The carrier bag slips from wrist to floor with a sinister
thud. Chapman smiles.

CUT TO:

INT - THE STRANGLER'S ARMS. A WEEK LATER.
A girl in a silver quilted puffa jacket treads a desolate
back street. A mini-cab passes-by, slows down. A mann at
struggles from the car with a guitar case. The girl walks
past. The musician barges through the door with his guitar.
Inside, a group of artists encircle a figure bathed in
uncanny light. The musician makes for the stage.
We arrive mid-conversation.

                    LUCIEN
          - HieronymousBosch? More like Hieronymousx
          xbloodyxbodge anonymous bloody bodge!
                    FELIX
          Shush! Let him speak! Go on.. you were saying?
                    CHAPMAN
          Well all I know is... If I want to make a
          painting of nothingness - I don't try and
          paint what nothingness 'looks' like, because
          nothing ness doesn't i'look' like anything...

Instead, I become 'blank' - then
the picture 'is' nothing...
Some of the artists proffer thoughtful nods.

                    LUCIEN
How fucking efficient! He merely thinks
of 'nothing' et voila... a painting of nothing
appears out of thin air!
                    MELANIE
    Well I think its quite refreshing.
                    FELIX
    So do I... think its refreshing.
                    LUCIEN
Oh, and you prefer witless sentiment?
                    MELANIE
    To sarcasm?
                    LUCIEN
    DO tell how you were blessed with such
    persipispicacious wisdom?

                    CHAPMAN
    In hospital.

                    LUCIEN
    I thought as much...

                    CHAPMAN
    in the morgue.

                    LUCIEN
    Oh dear...

                    CHAPMAN
It was there that I saw Life's flotsam
and jetsam washed up and reduced to meat
and bone. I realised then that the soul is deseased
... a disease gestated in the pit of the stomach,
rotting, putryfying - waiting for the jaws of
    maggots to set it free. It was there that I
    deedide-te- decided to rub humanity in its own vomit
    - to force it to look xt in the mirror.

                         FELIX
      You were allowed to work in the morgue?

                        CHAPMAN
     Not exactly. I did what I could when I could.
     But when they saw what I was doing they ridiculed
       me... they even destroyed my pictures.

                        MELANIE
           They destroyed your pictures?

                         LUCIEN
           That is rather harsh. Mind you,
           there's no higher accolade than
           utter rejection...
                         STACY
             give it a rest!
                        CHAPMAN
      The shrink said I had not talent. That I should
     give up painting and take up art therapy instead
       - for my own good.
                         FELIX
               What did you say?

                        CHAPMAN
            If thine eyes offend thee,
            pluck them out...
                         LUCIEN
               What?
                        CHAPMAN
            If thine eyes offend thee,
            pluck them out. So I pressed his
            eyeballs into the infertile gloom
            of his dreay mind.
     A moment of uneasy silence before collective affirmation
                          ALL
           PLUCK THEM OUT! PLUCK THEM OUT!
           PLUCK THEM OUT! PLUCK THEM OUT!

                    LUCIEN
          Fuck me! A righteous act of
          retribution! Buy the man a drink
          he must be bloody thirsty!
Chapman simmers with new found popularity. The artists
fall about laughing whilst poor Bubbles observes out of
earshot from the resentful other side of the bar.
Beneath Bubbles' chair, three cockroaches hidden by shadow
are similarly captivated by Chapman's epic tale.

                    PABLO
          What an inspirational story! That's it -
          I've made my mind up! I'm going to do what he
          did! Pursue my dream!

                    ROCHELLE
          Don't be absurd! Who's ever heard of a
          cockroach artist? They'll have your guts for
garters!
                    FATTY
          Don't listen to Rochelle. She's just jaded. You go
          for it Pablo - you, you got talent!

                    ROCHELLE
          Talent? Talent? You're so immersed in
          the theology of bullshit, you couldn't
          spot talent if it leapt up and bit you
          on the thorax!
                    FATTY
                 Woof!
                    ROCHELLE
                 Piss off!
Fatty continue to bicker whilst Pablo's earnest
ambition dimples into focus.

                    PABLO
          If I don't do it now, I never will...

On the stage, the lone musician begins to sing.

                    MUSICIAN
        Morning has broken, like the first
        morning, blackbird has spoken, like
        the first bird. praise for the singing,
        praise for the morning, mPraise for the sing
        ing fresh from the word....

From the grubby recesses.

                    FATTY
            Good luck old friend. I hope you
        find what you're looking for.

                    PABLO
        THXKKX Thanks Fatty...

                    ROCHELLE
        JESUS AND MARY WEPT! Pablo! Why d o
        you have to be iikx a nonconformist like
        everyone else? Why can't you just grub around
        with the rest of us in the safety of the
        shadows? What's so original about being
        unique?

                    PABLO
        But Rochelle, you know I've always wanted
        to be anartist - ever since I was knee-high to
    a grass-hopper!

                                        CUT TO:

Flash back to a young Pablo standing knee-high to a
grass-hopper. Thexgrasskxpperxraspsx Pablo is sketching
the grasshopper. The grasshopper rasps its back legs
together in appreciation. A bird swoops down and swallows
the grasshopper whole. Pablo throws his sketchbook to the
ground and wails out loud like a girl.

                                        CUT TO:

                    ROCHELLE
        You can't go You just can't...
                    PABLO
            Why?

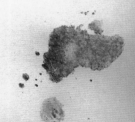

                    FATTY
              He's going...
                    ROCHELLE
              Why? Why? Can't you see?
              becquse I love you...
                    FATTY
              If you waīt to reach your dreamx
              Pbalo, there's your cloud! Floating away!
Pablo is now vigourously mating with Rochelle, while Fatty
watches the artist heading for the door. In the interim
between observing Chapman ax exit the p̶u̶b̶m̶a̶x̶i̶R̶x̶c̶h̶e̶l̶x̶ pub
Rochelle has birth to six healthy hungry newborn Pablo's
and is dutifully suckling all six.
                    ROCHELLE
              GO on... go...
Pablo scurries off in pursuit of the artist.
                    ROCHELLE
              - but don't expect me to piẃk up
              the pieces once the humans eat you
              up and spit you out!
                    MUSICIAN
              Sprung in completeness where his
              feet pass, Mine is the sunlight, mine
              is the mornig, born of the one light,
              Eden saw play...

                                            DISSOL

INT- STUDIO   s
Bubbles and Chapman have reigned from their daily group
crit to pick at brittle bagels and curdled curry. The ḋ
studio door opens and a female silhouette floats inside.
She moves with the precision of an assassin, b̶u̶t̶-̶d̶e̶v̶o̶i̶d̶-
o̶f̶-̶u̶r̶g̶e̶n̶c̶y̶ A neutral stare settles upon Chapman's x̶i̶t̶h̶x̶
withering husk. Bubbles leaps up to welcome the icy
ghoul into the warmth of the studio.
                    BUBBLES
              OO-oo-oo-aaaa-a-a-ee-o-Dora! Come in!
              Come in'. What brings you here to my
              humble abode? Oh... this is a friend,
              Chapman, he's sharing fo a bit, y'know
              helping out a fellow artist sort of thing.

DORA

(robotic)

Yes. I. KNOW. I came here to
meet him. In the flesh. I have heard
much about you MR Chapman. You are
forthright in your ideas. We are always
looking for alies. In. The. Fight. Against.
Mediocrity.

Bubbles deflates, resigned to the perfunctory part he has
to play in Chapmans' social ascendency.

BUBBLES

Dora's a post-humanist, aren't you Dora?

DORA

If you say so. Bubbles.

BUBBLES

Dora's a nihilist, aren't you Dora?

DORA

If you say so. Bubbles.

Doras hand rathet- ratchets out to Chapman who obliges with
his own dainty shake.

DORA

We live in lukewarm times. Imprisoned
within the mythologies of choice. The.
role. OF. The artist. Is. To. Wake. Us
from the anaesthesia of everyday life.
The. Past. Present. And. Future are merely
illusions constructed to tempt us with
unattainable goals. Therefore. Time is a
lie. Why Why
kill time when you can kill yourself?

CHAPMAN

. . . .

DORA

I am inviting you to an evening. Of.
performance and a post-performance
after-party. After the performances.

                    Tomoorow night. Please
                come. You too Bubbles.
                        CHAPMAN
                THANK YOU VERYmuch. May I
                ask what they're performing?
                        DORA
                Ha. Ha. Ha. Funny. Shall we say
                eight o'clock?
                        CHAPMAN
                I thought time was a lie...

                                        FAST FORWARD

EXT ♀ MAYFAIR MANSION. DOORSTEP.
Bubbles presses the doorbell.
                FEE FI FO FUM!
The door opens onto a diminutive dwarf dressd in giant's
garb.   BUTLER
                Mr Archie is expecting you.
                Please follow.
Inside, the receprion opens out onto an enormous art
gallery, dominated by a huge refrigerated bdock of ice
with a frozen polar bear being menaced by a shoal of
vicious penguins suspended in its core. Bu Bubbles can only
watch as Chapman scurries about like-a-special-child-in.He
is arrested before a painting of Adam and Eve spread-
eagled over broken crokery. He gasps at a vast canvas
with an ominous perspectival railway line covered in britt
brittle staxw straw with the words - DAS KAPITAL IST KAPUT-
JA? scrawled over in black bitumen. He sees a bright neon
sign that fizzes before switching between EAT and dEATh,
and a perfect stainless steel inflatable Golly Wog whose
immaculate mirror surface reflects his own primal wonderment. Peering xxxxxdinto the frozen POLAR OPPOSITES he
finds himself face-to-face with house owner and internati-
onal art collector, Mt Archie.
                        CHAPMAN
                I like your house...
                    ARCHIE
                    Quite.
Mr ARchie appears to be already dreessed for bed, in silk

dressing gown and slippers. Dora Enters from a side door.

                    MR ARCHIE
          Darling Dora! Oh, and Bubbles too!
          What xa charming surprise. How is the
          art world treating you these daya Bubbles?

                    BUBBLES
          Oooo-oo-o-ooo-oo-o-fine...
                    DORA
          This is Chapman.
                    MR ARCHIE
             Yes, we met. I'm glad you
             like my house.

Lead by little giant and big art collector, Chapman, Dora
and Bubbles enter the heavy floodgate double doors into
the fray. Dora intercepts a passing tray of champagne. She
hands an icy flute to Chapman, as he motions to thank her,
finds a bitter pill upon his tongue.

                    DORA
          Swallow. Trust. Me.

They weave through the guests until Doar and Archie are
sequestered into the mass, leaving Chapman and Bubbles to
fend for themselves.

                    MARTHA APPLEBAUM
             Dora! Giles! darlings. Come and mingle.
             Who's the weird looking insect with the
             monkey?
                    ARCHIE
             One of Dora's new projects.
                    MARTHA APPLEBAUM
                    Oh...

LATER...

The party is in full swing and Chapman is beginning to
fall foul of Doar's little party pill. He Circulatedxs
willynilly, party to peripheral snippets of converstation
. As the evening progressess he is prone to to halucination
s that force his tangential interactions with poets, artist
and writersk to take on an unwittingly profound significane
ce. The lights dim. A single spotlight picks out a simmer-
ing poet, leaning against a wal with indolent repose. There
are pockets of lazy applause. Everyone is almost excited.

POET

How the sun's
Holocaust doth
Deluge with
Indifference
Whilst solar beams
 Embalmed inside
 The skins
 Og the meek
who thus seek
A chance to find
An inherited share
 in immortality? Ha!
 Even the ocean vomits
Upon Darwin's shore
In the manner of
 A dog stealing chicken bones
 From its master's store
Bulimic tides
Conjvulse
and pulse –
Again and again
A monster tears at its
Throbbing teeth in vain
Yet not all
the earth's Asprin
Can cure the pain
Nor put Humpty Dumpty
Back together agaixn

There is applause. The poet sinks back into the loving
arms of obscurity.   LATER

Chapman is found ~~captive by~~ with a captive audience.

CHAPMAN
     – all I know is... if I'm doing a
     picture of notningness... I become nothing!
     Blank! See-through! Its as if I was never there!

An onlooker peels off to powder her nostril

                    GIRL
          IF i'm doing a picture of nothingness,
          I become nothing... genius, bloody
          genius.

Dora and Bubbles observe from afar.

                    BUBBLES
          Its strange. When this tormented stray
          first appeard on the scene he suffered
        crippling panic attacks at the mere mention of
        a private view. Now look! In a matter of
        months he's managed to conquered what I c
        couldnt manage to overcome in years.

                    DORA
          Bubbles. You are talented for a monkey. But
          . But.... but Chapman is... untimely. Itx
          sincerely wrenches the soul to witness first
          hand what forever elludes us mortals...

                    BUBBLES
        OO-oo-aa-ee-aa-oo-Dora! I do delieve you're
        defrosting! You havent seen his work. I honestly
        can't tell if he's a genius or mad, whatever it he
      is, it makes me feel like giving up.

                    DORA
          Poor sweet Bubbles. Jealousy is a terrible
          burden for a friend.

                    CHAPMAN
          Its tragic. I want to kill him and you want to
          fuck him!

                    DORA
          Two. Sides. Of. the. Same. Coin.

                                            CUT TO

Chapman is skt clawing his way up the grand stairs, using
his front teeth to pull on the carpet.

                    CHAPMAN
              NIhilism is not only despair
              and negation, but above all the
              desire to despair and negate ... TO DESPAIR!

AND NEGATE!

INT - STUDIO. A FEW DAYS LTER.

Chapman is lounging on the couch in unsavoury underpants,
channel-grazing daytime TV with petulant stabs at the remor
remote. Bubbles is trying to paint.

> BUBBLES
>
> For Christit's sake! Its difficult enough
> as it is... whyx aren't you working? What's wrong?
> You haven't painted a single roadkill for days!
> All you do is lounge about watching bloody
> daytime TV...

> CHAPMAN
> (below breath)
>
> Sanctimonious old flea bag.

Below the back-rest of the couch, Chapman takes aim at
Bubbles with the remote control.

> BUBBLES
>
> I don't undesratnd, you used to work
> religioo?oo-oo-aa-aa-ee-eeee--o-o-
> aa-aa-ee-eo-oo-oo-ooooo-ooo--ee-is it
> something I've said?Aa-oo-oo-ee-enough to
> drive me bloody mad!

Chapman is tickled by the unexpected effect of the remote.

> en   BUBBLES
>
> What's so funny?

> CHAPMAN
>
> Nothing...

> BUBBLES
>
> Oh whatever...

And with a slam of the door, Bubbles is gone.

FADE TO BLACK

A slab of blae darkness. The sound of the overground rumbl
rumbles close by.

A doorbell sounds. A muffles intercom co nverstaion downstairs before the buzzer x releasesx the door. A girl in xkt
silver puffa jacket stumbles into the darkness of the corridor. She fumbles for the lightswitch before staging her
perilous ascent, but before she sfaley reaches the top

step the timer times out and plunges her into gloom.
She stumbles on the very last step and a cascade of objects
fall from handbag to floor. A mobile phone bounces on the
grey floor and the screen saver illuminates a sickly baby
with sad sickly eyes.
Using the guiding light of the sickly baby's sad eyes, she
finds her way along the dark corridor.

                                              CUT TO:

Inside his room, G the studio Chapman listens to the
girl approach. The door handle rattles.

                    CHAPMAN
          Its open... just give it a shove.
The door bursts open and the girl totters inside, skin in
full agar bloom and hand outstretched with phone and sickly
baby with sad, sickly, demented eyes.

                    BUFFY
          Look! Its my little girl...
The track marks on her outstretched arm neatly synchron-
ise with the over-ground rumbling nearby. The light that

                    BUFFY
               gorgeous ain't she?

                                              CUT TO:

Concentrating on maintaining her verticality, Buffy
undresses whilst simultaneous relaying her popular tariff.
Chapman observes with impassive eyes.

                    BUFFY
          Handjob... a tenner. Blowjob... fifteen.
          Anal a nifty fifty... you can come in my
          mouth, on my tits, in my hair... over my face,
          or if you're after something a bit
          saucy you can just stick it up my vag...
          But I'll leave it up to you... I wouldn't
          want to ruin the moment.

                    CHAPMAN
          ...sit on the couch.

                                              CUT TO:

An uncanny panting sound invades the darkness.

PABLO
(wheezing)
...so far so good, so far so good...

Pablo pulls himself up onto the landing to find incandeseei
bright light shinnig forth from the gap beneath Gk the xim
studio door.

CHAPMAN
(muffled, inside the room)
I don't know if I can do it now!
I don't know how to make it come
without forcing it! I want it to flow
naturally, without faking it!

BUFFY
X J.st relax.. let it come on its ma own!

Pablo peers beneath the door.

xPabi PABLO
Its him... the artist!

CUT TO:

A brush dips into white spirit, swills around and clouds ta
the clear liquid blood-red. The brush stabs at the palette,
smearing paint with amateurish zeal before attacking the
fresh surface of the canvas.

We see BUffy's Olympia reclining on the couch, seen through
the distorting lens of the thinners jar.

CHAPMAN
That's it! Fuck appearances! Fuck resemblances!
fuck similarity! ExxintyBeat- Beauty is for
poodles! Oh now we're makin' bacon Buffy!
Oh remember this well Buffy, when you stare
into the abyss, the abyss laughs back at you!

Side-stepping the easle to scrutinize his model, Chapman's
enthusiasm instantly wanes.

CHAPMAN
Buffy? BUFFY? BUFFY?

Buffy is comatose, slumped out of pose and in narcoleptic
slumber. Chapman hovers hopelessely before his deflated
muse, aware of the impropriety of touching a naked girl
as she sleeps. He taps her shoulder, whispers in her ear.

                          CHAPMAN
               Buffy... Buffy? BUFFY? THIS IS YOUR
                  FATHER SPEAKING! WAKE UP! YOU'RE LATE
                  FOR SCHOOL!
Buffy stirs...
                           BUFFY
                     No Uncle-Buncle, I don't want to
                  stroke it anymore, I'm late for school....
                          CHAPMAN
               SHHHHHHHHHH! Its all right little one,
               Mummy's here! Go to sleep! Shhhh!
                           BUFFY
                   MUMMY? Zzzzzzz.....
She settles.

                          CHAPMAN
                  Now Mummy's going to move you a little bit...
Chapman manhandles Buffy back into the desired pose,
arranging her arms and legs in preferred composition.
                          CHAPMAN
                    There! Perfect!
Before returning to his easle he notices his hand is
covered in oil paint. He looks at Buffy. She has an
incriminating mottled handprint on her breast.

                                                CUT TO:

With cloth in hand Chapman endeavours to delicately remove
paint from Buffy's breast, the but the paint smears and
other colours magically appear before he realizes that the
cleaning cloth is contaminated.
He douses a new cloth with white spirit and sets to work.
Dubious jerking movements disturb Buffy's arm, now swing-
ing loose, until jerking gives way to Chapman's tongue, xx
working his waythrough the spectrum of rogue paint until
finding Buffy's nipple. There, Buffy wakes, opening her
eyes at the very moment that Chapman's sensually leaden
eyelids draw open.   CUT TO:
Buffy rages from the studio, slamming the door behind her
, naked, covered in paint and clutching her clothes.

She marches across the landing and hurls herself down the t
stairs.

> BUFFY
>
> You got more ~~ixxxxxble~~din' issues
> than a box of fucking Kleenex!
> (descending stairs)
> I shoul have known he was a wrong un'
> when he said he didn't want to fuck me!
> Bloody pervert! Kiddie-fiddler!
> Peado!

The light switch times_out and Buffy is plunged into darkness again, stumbling on the last step, the basement of all
insults -   BUFFY

> JEW!

                                CUT TO:

From the darkness outside Chapman's studio, ~~xxtx~~ Pablo
enters the gap and emerges this side with wonderment x
written on his cockroach face.

> ~~MORNINGXHAE~~
>
>   Morning has broken, like the first
>   morning, Blackbird has spoken, like
>   the first bird, Praise for the singing,
>   praise for the (etc)
>
>   PABLO
>
> Look! Burnt umber! Cadmium red!
> Here a palette knife... there a
> tube of ultramarine blue! A hog hair
> brush! Paint rags! Oh the unmistakable
> scent of turpentine! (spxlutters).. it
> is! Its a studio! A real-life artist's
> garret! I've arrived! I've bloody-well
> made it!

Pablo dissapears under the battered studio couch and emerg
emerges the other side, aware of a strange grunting coming
from above. However, his primary attention is directed to
the painting before him - now turned to face the couch

where Buffy lay in repose. Upon the easel's wooden mantle
a monstrouslxy deformed nude.

> PABLO
>
>> What a axxxx nauseating picture!
>> Revolting! Sickening! What could have
>> possibly inspired anyone to create such a
>> misshapen specimen? Surely its not the
>> function of art to wallow in filth for
>>> filth's sake, to paint the human being
>>> in a state of putrefaction?

The grunting from above is increasing in intensity.
Pablo dares to look up.

> VOICE FROM ABOVE
>
>> UH... UH... UH...monkey's coming!
>> Monkey's coming! Monkey's coming!
>
> PABLO
>
>> OH NO!

An opalescent string of sticky white xpxxkxgxxkxxxfx stuff
falls through the air, tangling in slow motion before
landing on Pablo, enveloping the poor insect in deadly
human DNA. Pablo struggles to escape the letahl- lethal
meniscus, and his voice can be heard gurgling...
Suddenly, the studio door bursts open and Bubbles enraged
Bubbles rushes in screeching like an injured gorilla.
Chapman leaps to his feet snatching at his pants, hopping
on the spot to arrange his modesty whilst simultaneously
gesturing to the top of his head.

> CHAPMAN
>
>> BUBBLES! You need to re-tune! Re-tune!
>
> BUBBLES
>
>> Ooo-oooo-o-o-oee-ee-aa-!

Beneath Chapman's hopping foot the unmistakable sound of
xxxx crushed exoskeletal chitin.

> BUBBLES
>
>> Oo-oo-aq-aa-aa-oh sorry!

Bubbles has his little suitcase on his bed and is packing

and some bananas for the journey.

> BUBBLES
>
> That's it! I've had enough!
> I'm packing it in... I can't kid
> myself anymore, I'm just not cut out
> to be an artist. I'm going back to my old
> job - if they'll have me.

> CHAPMAN
>
> Packing it in? You daft apeth - you can't
> just give it up!

Chapman sneaks a peak beneath his foot to find the
unexplainable mess of broken cockroach and semen.

> BUBBLES
>
> Nobody is interested in my kind of
> work. Its not ugly enough. Its got nothing
> to do with say about death or decay or pain
> or the fucking human condition...

> CHAPMAN
>
> But what will I do without you? What
> about all your paintings? You can't just walk
> out on all your work!

> BUBBLES
>
> Yes I can and I am! They're yours now!
> burn them or paint over them, do what
> you want with them. I don't care.

> CHAPMAN
>
> Oh come on Bubbles! Lets get a takeaway
> some beer, you'll forget about it after a
> Balti Chicken Rogon... with your favourite
> ba-na-na-frit-ters...?

> BUBBLES
>
> I HATE CURRY! ALWAYS HAVE!

And with that, and a slam of the door, Bubbles is gone.

> DISSOLVE TO

INT ? CHAPMAN STUDIO, DAYS LATER.

Chapman is lounging on the couch watching daytime TV.
A knock at the door.

> CHAPMAN
> I told you - I'll get you the bloody
> rent when that crook Bubbles sends me
> the money he owes me.

Martha Applebaum and Roberto enter.

> CHAPMAN
> Who are you? You can't just barge in...

> ROBERTO
> oh I'm sure you won't mind having Martha
> Applebaum in your studio...

                                    CUT TO:

Chapman is frantically washing chipped tea cups in the
make-shift kitchen segregated by a curtain.

> APPLEBAUM
> May we look around?

> CHAPMAN
> Well if you just wait (scrubbing)...
> I'll be... one second... and then I
> can show you...

The visitors are browsing nonetheless.

> APPLEBAUM
> What do you think?

Applebaum is holding up a small canvas. Chapman reverses
backards through the curtain to protect the tea on the tray

> APPLEBAUM
> Such verve... so raw.

Chapman abandons the tray on the table, and as if to concur
with Applebaums comments, snatches up a small canvas to
observe his own talent. Roberto is thus drawn to the same
painting, and in a moment of unwitting slapstick choreog
choreography, both Chapman and Roberto have their backs to
Applebaum, whose comments are anyway addressed to Bubble's
paintings on the opposite side of the studio.

                    CHAPMAN
        This is an early roadkill work.
        I'm still in my roadkill period.
        I think there's still life in the
        pr oject yet.
                    Roberto
                I can see why...
                    APPLEBAUM
        I suppose there is something
        quite animalistic about them...
                    CHAPMAN
            Well, there would be.
                    ROBERTO
            Clearly.
                    APEL APPLEBAUM
            But I love how the childish
            handprints manage to marry the humourous
            with the heavyweight... Its almost as if
            gestural painting has collided with
            conceptualism... a kind of conceptual
            expressionism... conundrumism!

Chapman and Roberto peer deeper into the painting of the
squashed ginger cat.

                    CHAPMAN
            Handprints? Conundrumism?

Chapman finds Applebaum pawing over the stack of Bubbles'
cast-offs. He discards his canvas into Roberto's willing
hands.   ROBERTO
                    (oblivious)
            ...its so bad, its good. Its so
        fuck-you and yet have a nice day!
                    CHAPMAN
                NO WAit a minute... not those...
                    APPLEBAUM
            Oh don't be bashful Mr Chapman,
            modesty is such a waste of time.

                    CHAPMAN
        Let me explain. These paintings over here
        are not actually mine. They xxxewere given
        to me - they were a gift.
                    APELBAUM
    Talent as rare as this has to be a gift.
                    CHAPMAN
        That's not what I meant. They're mine in
        so far as they belong to me, but they're not mine.
                    APPLEBAUM
    I agree. They belong to humanity -
        to the collective struggle - or
    whoever has enough money to purchase them!
                    CHAPMAN
        What about this one! (grabbing the
        canvas from Roberto). This one
        really struggled!
                    APPLEBAUM
        Idiotic.
                    ROBERTO
        The missing link! Attention seeking
        rubbish! Shock for shock's sake!
                    CHAPMAN
        How bloody dare you!
                    AppleBAUM
    Your loyalty to the imbecile who
    perpetrated these atrocities is touching, but
    you should be careful that your ailing friend
        doesn't suck you backwards into the gloomy
        xxxxxxx cave where I assume he resides.
        Has anyone else seen this work?
                    CHAPMAN
                    No.
                    APPLEBAUM
        XXX You've done your work - now
        let me do mine. How many pictures are
        there?

                    CHAPMAN
        Well there's about twenty or thirty of
    those - and forty-three of these...

                    APLLEBAUM
            Very funny. I assume you're short of
                cash?

                    CHAPMANS
                So?

                    APPLEBAUM
            Shall we say ten thousand pounds -
            as an advance against sales?

                    CHAPMAN
                Ten thousand pounds?

                    APPLEBAUM
                Fine. Fifteen then.

                    CHAPMAN
                I suppose true genius is the
                bedfellow of chance - and anyway,
                you can't meddle with fate!

                                        DISSOLVE

    INT ? EVENING. STRANGLER'S ARMS.
    Chapman is hunched in the dingy back bar of the Strangler's
    Arms, nursing the dregs of a drink. He barely manages to k
    lift head to acknowledge some artist friends enter the pub
    already knee-deep in worthy conversation. Chapman sinks
    another notch into the mi re of self-pity.

                    CHAPMAN
                How the hell did I end up incriminated
                by the false accusation of genius? His work confus
                ed for mine - mine eclipsed by his. Well, if
                Marth Applebaum insists on having a chimp for
                her circus - then its a chimp she shall have.
                If its a tormented artist they want, what
                better than one wracked with guilt?
                The paintings aren't mine but the angst is.

DORAx DORA

Destiny. Beckons.

CHAPMAN

Oh god... you've heard.

DORA

Everybody knows. I called by the studio.
Tried to telephone. Where. Have. You.
been?

CHAPMAN

Busy.. just busy with this big,
stupid mistake.

DORA

Only you would greet success with contempt.
Can I come up and see your etchings. An innocent
peak. Before you. Are. Too. famoué to indulge the
likes of me.

INT - UPSTAIRS

Upstairs, the studio door swings open with a drunken shove.
Bubbles' paitings dominate the studio. Chapman's road-
kill paingtings are nowhere to be seen.
Chapman makes for the WC. Dora shouts over the sound of
his hit and miss urine.

DORA

I'm assuming you cleared Bubbles' work out.
Its for the best. Poor chimp. I wonder what
he's up to now?

CHADMAN

Science.

DORA

What?

CHAPMAN

(fluxifl flushing)
FLMX SCIENCE!

Dora ambles the lengths of the studion studying the-paintig
the picturess.

DORA

As a rule. I find. Painting. Self-

                     indulgent. Wrapped up with
                  sybaritic emotions. Navel-gaving.
               Nothing. Of. Interest.... But these...
               these are different... did you paint them
               left handed? I love how you use the
               inaccuracy of your hand - the dumbness is
             so refreshing... the beautiful handprints...
            the pretty colours, so... so positive... so
            life affirming, just lovely, so human!
Dora is imploring Chapman with an earnestness ill-befitting
her nihilistic countenance.

                          CHAPMAN
                   Human? HUMAN? I'LL SHOW
                 YOU EXACTLY HOW HUMAN THEY ARE!
Chapman launches on the nearest canvas, putting his foot
through, tearing the canvas and splitting the wooden
stretcher and thus becoming entangled in the collapsed
structure.

                          CHAPMAN
             There you go! NOW ITS BLOODY HUMAN!
Dora is speechless. Chapman has exhausted himself, now
snared in Bubbles' painting. But the violent outburst fails
to elicit the desired effect. Instead, Dora is so moved to
lug lunge forward and smother Chapman's face with a shaol
of wet kisses. Hopelessly tangled, he struggles to fend off
Dora's attack.

                          CHAPMAN
                    Get off! Get off me!
Dora draws back aghast like the last wave before the tsuna
tsunami.

                          DORA
                 I thought that you....
                          CHAPMAN
                 What? What did you think?
                          DOXRA
                 You don't know? You can't tell?
                          CHAPMAN
                 Tell? Tell what exactly?
                          DORA
                 That I love you!
                          CHAPMAN
                 Love? Love is for Poodles!

Dora makes for the door, pursued by Chapman, howling and
barking, still ensnared in Bubbles' painting. Dora gushes
down the stairs in floods of tears. Leaning over the
bannisters -

                    CHAPMAN
          You don't want me! You want the monkey!
          THE BLOODY MONKEY! You all do - you
          just don't know it yet!

                                        DISSOLVE TO

INT ? CRACK DEN. NIGHT.

Three bumper-sized lines of white powder decorate a glass
coffee-table. The table jerks with female sniggering, plus
male grunting. Drug detritus dances on the periphery of
the table and a bottle of poppers with muscle-man logo
teeters on the edge before leaping to the carpet. A face
savaged my amphetamines leans forward with rolled note in
mostril. She lines up the noteyxhui- the note up at the kx
beginning of the most abundant striation, but before in-
haling, recieves an unholy shunt from behind, naturally
causing the girl to exhale, and thus the white powder to
billow into thin air.

                    BUFFY
          For fuck&'s sake, you stupid twat!
          You made me blow it all over the fucking
          carpet!
                    DAWN
          Don't fret Buffy. Either the gentleman
          coughs up enough filthy for another bag
          of gak sharpish, or he shall find himself
          removed from our humble abode, and thus
          forgoe the pleasure of our delightful company.
                    CHAPMAN
          I do apologize dear ladies. I don't know
          what came over me.
                    BUFFY.
          I do. Its running down my leg.

The girls cackle like popcorn. Chapman recovers his spent
trousers and extracts a fistful of crisp twenties.

>   CHAPMAN
>   Here. Money for old rope. Thank Christ
>   for Martha Applebaum! Wp Onwards fair
>   ladies! Qnwaxxd On to the crack of Dawn!
>   DAWN
>   You can be up my crack all day —
>   as long as you can fucking pay!
>   BUFFY
>   Dawn, you're a fucking poet!

Buffy sniffs, Dawn and Chapman take their turn. Once the
poppers have taken their toll, sexual positions rotate in
a glacial trance. Chapman's rictus grimace remaingng
constant throughout each stupified tantric manouvre.
Suffice to say, it has the appearance of the rarest of
sloth gang bangs.

>   DISSOLE TO

INT - EVENING. CHAPMAN'SXX SOLO EXHIBITION OPENING AT
MARTHA APPLEBAUM GALLERY.
Chapman is a corpse, animated by the enthusiasm of others.
Buffy and Dawn do their utmost to keep the artist upright
as they push through the queue for the gallery entrance.
Inside, a banner announces the name of the show.

>   INTOSPASTIC; FROM THE BLACKENED BEYOND

>   EWEROBERTO
>   Bubbly anyone?
>   CHAPMAN
>   Oh how guilt resigns to the sound
>   of a supersonic cork...

Insdie In the gallery, the pristene elite sparkle with
effervescent chatter. Bubbles' paintings are hung with
humbling xeverance, each singularity absorbing chit-chat
with stellar confidence.

>   BOY
>   What do you think?

                    GIRL
        I like the titles.
                    BOY
        'The wrong man', 'Double bind',
        'Catch-22', 'Mistaken identity!..
        Wha**t** do youthink he's trying to say?
Ulrich pushes into the picture.
                    ULRICH
        Its-like ze Columbine with crayons!
                    GIRL
        Does that mean you approve?
                    ULRICH
        Ja! Anyone who makes ze splishy-splashy
        angst painting unt names it 'I didn't paint
        this picture' is ze genius in my book. You
        know, ze mind is like ze parachute - it doesn't
work unless its open. I think zis Chapman's mind is wide
                    open.
                                        CUT TO:
Martha **A**pplebaum can hardly contain herself in her car-
crash Issey Miyake.

                    APPLEBAUM
            How convenient. The work seems to
            appeal to the intelligentsia because its
            edgy, and the ignorant because it pretty...
                    ROBERTO
        Let's hope it has the s**maa a** smae effect
        on the collectors.
                    APPLEBAUM
        You're so fucking cynical sometimes
        Roberto. Where is my artist? Speak of
            the devil.
Chapman plants a kiss on Applebaum**s**s hand.
                    APPLEBAUM
        So g**aa**i glad you could make it.
        You scrub up **n**icely. Overnight success
        suits you!

                    CHAPMAN
          Well if the shoe fits...
                    ROBERTO
          I thought Irony was dead.
                    CHAPMAN
          No, its like sentience, once you
          know you're going to die, you can't
          help joking about it.
                    APPLEBAUM
          Walk with me,... I'm sure you'll
          be over the moon when I tell you its already
          a pormographic success. I could have sold each
          piece ten times over. We need more. Pronto!
Ah! Let me introduce you to thex David and
Lauzra Gibbons. They're from lynchburg, Virginia.
Beau is a -
BETXX Beyond the Gibbons, Chapman notices Dora staring at
him from across the gallery. She has an insinuating frxmx
frown.

                    APPLEBAUM
          (whispering)
            Before your cock leads you
            completely astray, let me introduce you
            to... Gilxtx Giles! Nice to see you!
                    ARCHIE
          Mr Chapman. A real pleasure to
          see you this side of success! I
          hope you'll forgive my greed, but I've
          earmarked a few of the best pictures.
The Gibbons deflate.
                    ARXIQH ARCHIE
            Perhaps you could come to the house
            and oversee thx your hang.
                    CHAPMAN
            Yes, I'd like that. I'd like
            to come to the kxxxx house and
            oversee myself hang.

APPLEBAUM

Be nice... what's wrong?

CHAPMAN

Nothing, other than the fact
that these are not my paintings.

Apllebaum seizes Chapman's arm and leads him away.

APPLEBAUM

Idon't know what's got into you or what
little game you're playing, but let me tell you,
I'm them organ grinder, and you're the monkey.
If you insist on coming apart at the seams tonight
I shall be forced to grind your organ. Now smile...
you're being adored.

Dora has disappeard. But Dawn and B^{U}ffy are loitering near
'The wrong man', eager to attract Chapman's attention.

CHAPMAN

You asked for it...

Chapman nods. The girls lift 'The wrong man' from the wall
to reveal behind a diminutive study of a flattened ginger
cat. Dawn and Buffy assist the painting's public exposure
with gestures of the hip and hand.

CHAPMAN

I presnint present... 'Road-kill number one!'

The gallery is aghast. Buffy and Dawn move swiftly to
the next canvas, and with gemmx uncommon aplomb, repeat
the action - capitalising on the collective paralysis.
Thus they are able to remove the next canvas without
interference, carefully propping it to one side in order x
that another road-kill canvas can be revealed to all and
sundry beneath.

CHAPMAN

'Road kill number two'.

Before Dawn and Buffy can execute their intervention on
the third canvas, the momentary freeze shatters and the
crowd are now animated by mocking laughter. Sidew are split
and pants soiled. Even Buffy and Dawn are contaged by laug
laughter, relenting to the torrent of mirth.

Chapman is at firt horrified before being obliterated.
Applebaum steps forward, clapping purposefully.
The crowd fall silent.

> APPLEBAUM
>
> Not content to rest upon the laurels
> of talent, he seeks to mock our beourgeois
> adulation with these... these sublime errors
> of judgement! Never before have I witnessed a
> performance hidden within a painting exhibition.
> Chapman, I stand in awe! I applaud you!

The crowd are moved to applause too.

> APPLEBAUM
> (whispering)
> Christ! Is nothing sacred? When I said
> those paintings didn't deserve to see the
> light of day, I didn't mean for you to
> crucify the poor oaf in public! I hope
> your missing link is not here - for his
> sake!

Whilst Applebaum ushers Roberto to replace the original
paintings, Dora blemishes Chapman's sight once once more,
staring at him from across the gallery. But now she is
mouthing somtheing.

> DORA
> I know what you've done....

DISSOLVE TO:

EXT/INT ST. JOHN BAR AND RESTAURANT. EVENING
Chapman decants from a black cab and enters the restaurant,
adjsuting himself before taking aim through the packed dining room.
He finds Applebaum and Roberto and slumps opposite with
unrepentant attitude. He confiscates Roberto's wine, downs
it in one and displaces a single full-bloodied burp, with
velvety tannins and a long, subtle yet rich, fruity finnish

> APPLEBAUM
> I took the liberty of ordering
> your rolled pig's spleen and chips.

Roberto and I have eaten.

ROBERTO

- and partially digetsed.

APPLEBAUM

So now the dust has settled I
thought we should de-brief.

ROBERTO

The exhibition was a xxxxx great
success. Collectors are begging to
see new work.

CHAPMAN

Well there's a sucker born
every minute.

APPLEBAUM

Well before you soil your underpants
in excitement, I need to know when we
can have more work - or at least see it.
You have been working?

CHAPMAN

Can't stop. But what's the hurry?
You've flooged thex other stuff so
we can afford to take a breather.

ROBERTO

Or make hay while the sun shines?

CHAPMAN

Or give up while the going's good?

ROBERTO

Or strike while the xxxxx iron's hot?

CHAPMAN

Good things come to those that wait.

ROBERTO

Faint heart never won fair lady.

CHAPMAN

Slowly, slowly, xxxxx catchy monkey! SHIT!
SHIT! SHIT! Well anyway, I'm taking a sabbatical!

Roberto spits his drink out.

> ROBERTO
>
> A what?

> APPLEBAUM
>
> He wants to retire and take up
> scrabble.

The waiter arrives with Chapman's spleen.

> CHAPMAN
>
> Whiskey?

> WAITER
>
> My mistake...

> APPLEBAUM
>
> If we could just keep you from your coma
> a moment longer, I'll tell you the amazing
> news. You..... You're going to represent
> Britain at the Venice Biennale!

> ROBERTO
>
> What do you think of that?

Chapman is blank.

> ROBERTO
>
> The British pavillion is yours!

> CHAPMAN
>
> But I've only done one exhibition!
> I haven't even got a pssport! Anyway,
> you can't award pavillions to artists -
> its a compulsion, not an Olympic event!
> An internal malaise transferred to the outside,
> not a sport!

> APPLEBAUM
>
> We need new paintings. Brand new and now.

> CHAPMAN
>
> But I8m not quite ready to -

At the window, Dora is peering in. She begins banging on
the glass.

                    DORA
        I know what you've done!
        I know what you've done!
        I know what you've done!
                    APPLEBAUM
    What did you do?
                    CHAPMAN
    Nothing compared to waht I'm going to do.
            GARCON!
The waiter arrives to deliver a black permanent marker
on a silver kidney dish. Chapman scrawls his signature
on the table cloth.
                    WAITER
        That'll do nicely sir.

                                DISSOLVE TO

INT - SEARING WHITE INFINITY SPACE CURVE.
Chapman is naked, perfoming uncomfortable gestures of
genital shame, cowering in the ~~corner~~ straw-bedded corner
of a large cage. A neural implant protrudes from an
irritated hole in the crown of his head.
                GORILLA PENROSE
        Hey monkey boy!
                    CHAPMAN
        Oo-oo-aa-ee-oo-oo-aa-oo?
                GORILLA READ
        The great Homo Sapiend. For all its
        art, science and religion - offended by
        its own nature!
                    CHAPMAN
        Oo-oooo-aaa-a-a-a-a?
                GORILLA FRY
        Dignity! Ha!
                GORILLA GOMBRICH
        Man is such a hive of parasites
        that it is doubtful whether his body
        is not more theirs than his...

He throws Chapman a banana. Chapman wakes, sits up in bed
scratches his head, pinches an imaginary tick between
finger and thumb before examining it and eating it. He
gets out of bed and goes downstairs to the studio.

                                            CUT TO:

Blank canvases are propped against each wall of the
impressive purpose-buit artist's studio. Chapman shuffles
before one of the canvases.   CUT TO:

                    CHAPMAN
            Brand new work. Now?nHow difficult
            can it be?

                                            CUT TO:

                    CHAPMAN
                (reading aloud)
            The modern artist expresses an inner
            world of energy, motion, and force...
            it doesn't make much difference how the
            paint is put on. Technique is just a means
          of arriving at a statement... you should not
        be aware of what you are doing until you are fi-
            nished... do not fear making changes... or
            destroying the picture... life of its own own..
Chapman hunches... swings his arms, scratches and grunts.
he begins to paint.

                    CHAPMAN
              BE a monkey... oo-aa-o-
              aa-oo-oooo-oo-o-eee-ee-its
              only when you lose contact with the
              painting that the result is a mess...
              ooo-oo-oo-aa-aaa-eea bit of give and take
              and the painting comes out well...
He stops. Steps back to a take stock, now standing erect.
Time to inspect the effects of his momentary descent.
                    CHAPMAN
              Oh you can't monkey with the truth!

The paint brush falls to the floor in slow motion.

EXT/INT - PITCH BLACK

Darkness. We hear the shuffling of uncomfortable animals.
The sound of animals whimpering in terrible discomfort and
pain.

A small explosion precipitates acacophany of animal shrieks
A door bursts open. Two flashlight beams cough through the
smoke. A hand ~~fumbks~~ fumbles for a light switch inside the
broken doorframe. Flourescent tubes burst across the ~~sxiki~~
sunken ceiling like photon torpedoes, revealing cages ~~xtak~~
stakked from floor to ceiling occupied by rabbits, mice, c
cats, dogs, and rats in various states of surgical
rectification. Melamine workstations are plagued by test-
tubes, autoclaves, chemical containers. Biohazard signs
warn that this is a top secret dirty tricks research -
laboratory.

The insurgents remove the brown paper bags from their heads
Dora and Chapman begin to search the corridors of cages,
finding a weeping white rabbit, a sad cat with implant on
its chest, a miserable dog with internal organs set on
the outside of its body, a cheerless rat with a manifold ~~sk~~
cluster of syringes taped into its stomach. A beagle is ~~st~~
strapped to leather retraints smoking a cigarette (Chapman
steals a quick drag).

They find the limp body of their dear friend Bubbles
cracified to a cruel scaffold. His eyes are stapled to the
table and nerves pinned to infinity.

                    DORA
          OH BUBBLES! What have they done to you?
          How could they do this? Helpme Chapman,
          Help me set him free!

Chapman has found a pharmiceutical cabinet.

                    CHAPMAN
          Fentanyl... Buprenorphine... Propofol
          Halopern... Who'd have thought! So many
          painkillers in a vivisection lab! Must
          be saving them for a rainy day! Aha!
          Pethadine! Bingo!

DORA

What are you doing? Hurry!
~~Help~~ We don't have much time!
Help me get Bubbles off this
evil contraption!

Chapman punctures the rubber fontanelle on the top of the
small amber bottle - so coloured to ensure that harmful
background UV radiation is sfaley absorbed and sensitive
medicines stored inside are not tainted. He draws the
opioid analgesic up into the syringe before plunging the
business end into Dora's pretty nape. She manages a sweet
quizzical expression before crumpling to the floor.
Chapman's curiosity releases one of the staples mooring
Bubbles' left eye to the table. The elastic sinew snaps the
monkey's eyeball back into its socket. It blinks. Chapman
releases the other displaced orb into its hungry hole.
Now that Dora is snug-as-a-bug-on-a-drug, Chapman is free
to examine the sketches and diagrams scattered about ~~Bubbl~~
Bubbles' workstation. He discovers books on monkey-art,
rudimentary colour charts and poster-painted handprints
on calibarted graph paper. He quickly surmises that the
experiments being conducted upon his friend are most
likely of a neuroesthetic category. To wit, a clipboard
confirms his suspicions:

Despite the changes that occur
when Bubbles processes visual stimuli,
his brain has the ability to retain
knowledge of the constant and essentisl
properties of an object and discard
irrelevant dynamic properties. This applies
not only to the ability to always see a
banana as the colour yellow, but also the
recognition of faces at varying angles.
much of this neural functioning has been
attributed to the visual areas of Bubbles'
brain - specifically the V1 cortex and the
Specialized groups of cells which fire for

a specific orientation stimulus.
Interestingly, there is a significant
difference in the pattern of Bubble's
brain activity when viewing abstract art
as opposed to representational art.
In a study using filtered forms of
abstract and representational art,
Bubbles8 bilateral occipital gyri,
his left cingulate sulcus and bilateral
fusiform gyrus showed increased
preference when viewing abstract art.
However, this preference may be caused
by the large processing requirments placed
upon the visual system when Bubbles was
exposed to high levels of visual detail in
artwork such as Goya's etchings...

Bubbles is wired up to a big machine with an array of
dials arranged around on oscillator scope. Simple curiosity
sees fit to twist one of the knobs and Bubbles' sad face
ä suddenly lights up with a friendly grimace and a
twitching of the right arm. With ~~further~~ an adjustment
the ape's arm is possessed by a phantom sketching motion.
Chapman is compelled to place a Biro in the monkey's grip
plus paper beneath ~~itx~~ the pen. He engages the dial and
the oscillator grits its sharp teeth, but Bubbles' ensuing
scribble is at best childish, and worst, of no use to ~~anyan~~
anyone.
Chapman selects another dial setting at random and a
semblance of order magically takes hold in the form of a
primitive stic k man. An astonishing graphic evolution
yet cut short by the unwelcom wail of Police sirens.

                                        CUT TO:

With dear friend swaddled safe in a blanket, Chapman
stumbles through the research facility's woodland
boundary. Not far behind, barking dogs and chaotic torch
beams seek out their quarry. Yet the sound of rustling

leaves follows close on Chapman's heels. Mainting forward
motion, he twists his head to gain sight of his pursuer,
but nothing materialises. Keeping pace alongside Chapman is
a mouse with a human eye firmly grafted onto its back, and
then another rodent laden with a human nose - also fleeing
an uncertain fate in the lab. In fact, one-by-one, a whole
host of oppurtunist mice stream past, collectively burdened
by the essential organs of an entire man, whose mouth-mouse
is just now running parallel and forms a smile, even
exhhanges a convivial pleasantry before speeding ahead.

                                        CUT TO:
INT - CHAPMAN'S APARTMENT.
Bubbles is asleep in Chapman's bed. Nurse CHapman is in
impatient attendance.

                    CHAPMAN
              Bubbles! Bubbles! Its your
              favourite! Banana soup!
              Yummy num-nums!
Bubbles upens a single bloodshot eye.

                                        CUT TO:
Poert-Chapman conveys Bubbles in a rusty wheelchair,
the monkey wearing a dressing gown and holding his hairy
hands over sore eyes. Inside the studio, a number of i
luxuary-grade canvases are leant against the walÃs. Brand
new brushes, fresh paint and mixing buckets are all within
easy reach.

                    CHAPMAN
              You can open your eyes now!
                    BUBBLES
          OO-OOOOO-AAAAAAAA-AA-AA-EEEEE-EE-
          AA?oOO-OO-OO-OOO-AAA-EEEE!!!!!!!
                    CHAPMAN
              Oh don't even go there! I'll
              explain later. I have to pop out
              for a bit... shan't be long. You
              just occupy yourself a bit...

Chapman exits, casting ~~anxious~~ a hopeful glance behind.

> CHAPMAN
>
> Treat the place as you would your
> own...

CUT TO:

INT - STUDIO, EVENING

Chapman returns. Tiptoeing in the dark, tipsy with ~~with~~
excitement.

> CHAPMAN
>
> Oh Bubbles? Oh Bubbles...
> Where are you?

When the lights flickerka on, Chapman beholds the sight of
colourful fishing boats, bathetic landscapes, frolicking
foals, wistful flowers, tearful children and puppy dogs.

Chapman is haunted by Applebaum's invocation...

> APPLEBAUM
>
> We need new work... brand new...
> paintings... soooooooooooooon!

CUT TO:

INT - KITCHEN. MORNING.

Chapman is hard at work creating a machine composed of a
cascading aggregate of doemstic compnents, incorporazting
amongst other things, a microwave, Black and Decker work-
mate, toaster, blender, garlic crusher, cheese gzzter and
Henry the Hoover.

CUT TO:

INT - STUDIO. LATE MORNING

Once Bubbles is settled into the Eames recliner modified
with triple strength velcro restraints, Chapman presses
Henry's big red button and Bubbles' eyes bulge bigger and
redder than the button. His body convulses and the implant
atop his head begins to glow before smouldering with acrid
smoke. Nonetheless, the hairy mitt in question scribbles
frantically upon the pad of paper set beneath his hand,
such that the pen bound to his spasmic grip is swiftly
ground to a plastic mush.

With a number of adjustments and a replacement Biro, the
experiment progresses until the pad sets beneath Bubbles'
charred hand evidences a primal stick-man equal in kind to
the ~~imgaexx~~ image produced in the lab.

> CHAPMAN
> Almost there, my intrepid friend!
> Hold tight!

The machine hums and Bubbles stinks. His balck fur smould-
dering whilst his hand is spurred on by the relentless
direct current. He draws a three-dimensioanl snow man with
hat, carrot and twig, plus small pieces of coal for ~~fxxtux~~
facial features. Chapman is getting the hang of his machine
and is pleased that Bubbles' shading is getting better, and
his cross-hatching is coming on a storm. He makes a few ~~xd~~
adjustments and resumes.

> CHAPMAN
> That's it BUBbles! Nearly there!
> One final push and I think we'll
> have the right kind of stuff and
> then everything will be alright!

Once again, ~~the~~ electricity fizzes ~~xkxnfx~~galong every neur
al pathway in Bubbles' hardening body. He even appears to
be outlining the basic shapes of a human portrait.
Chapman holds his breath knowing that abstraction won't
be too far behind. Bubbles is biting his tongue, such that
Chapman is moved to disengage the input source. Spots of
blood have spoilt the uncanny likeness of Brad Pitt on the
pad set beneath the monkey's singed paw.

> CHAPMAN
> No, non, no! I want the other
> stuff. The stuff you did before
> you left!

> BUBBLES
> ~~Ixknaxt~~(exhausted)
> I know, you keep saying that...
> but I've told you, I don't remember
> anything from before!

Chapman's irritation fiddles some more, adjusting
both ends of the experimental collision, with screwdriver.
Satisfied that his fiddling is good, he presses on.
Once more Bubbles&xt eyes pop, and the phantom hand begins.
The image magically vivisected into being this time
is.... Danny Devito!

                    &xxp CHAPMAN
                  What?! Where's all this
                  coming from? You don't even
                  watch television!

Like this, Chapman's persistence is rewarded by an
unbridled stream of uncanny likenesses of John Travolta,
Julia Roberts, Tom Hanks, Sandra Bullock and Tom Cruise,
before Chapman unplugs the monkey in disgust.

                                        CUT TO:
                    CHAPMAN
                  If you want something done,
                  do it yourself....

Freshly showered with towel around his neck and a glass
of milk in his left hand, Bubbles observes Chapmann with
anode and cathode in each hand. He has wheeled the machine
next to one of the large canvases leant against the wall.
He attatches the alligator clips to the lobes of his ears,
takes a modest sized brush in his right hand which he dips
in xxdxpxixt black paint. He draws a deep breath and with
his left hand flicks Henry on.

Chapman'ns convulsions are reminiscent of pioneering ECT
experiments conducted upon the bodies of criminals and
the insane, whose spasms were violent enough to snap
thxxx their spines. Hence Chapman misses the canvas
altogether.

                                        CUT TO:

Chapman has a juicy black eye.

CUT TO:

INT – STUDIO. CHAPMAN IS HARD AT WORK ON
HIS OWN PART OF THE JAKE AND DINOS
CHAPMAN EXHIBITON AT WHITE CUBE IN JULY.

The object vacillates before him as though its sensate surface
is connected to a greater more complex nervous system within.
He cannot put a finger upon the specifics of its uncanny
disposition for fear of being contaged by touch – as if it were
a thin shell endangered by exterior sources of scepticism, a
precarious crust or alien fontanel ready to collapse at the
mere suggestion of its substantive integrity being in question
– a subordinate realm of immanent disintegration – in short,
a seething gobbet of pure madness, shorter still, c-h-a-o-s... As
though hell-bent on inviting catastrophe, he picks up his
round-ended scissors and begins to cut, cut, cut into the damn
cardboard, cut into it, cut, cut, cut, snip, snip, snip, make it
sing out for him to stop! Now the glue. Glue, glue, glue,
stick, stick, stick! Stick the pieces together, odds and ends, ends
and odds! Mad shapes brought into being by reckless scissor!
Cosmic hurricanes spray out into the void, shatter the space,
burst with immeasurable force of the imaginary upon quaking
towers. Rhomboidal, opalescent, shimmering arches sink
upward to unattainable zeniths. Tumbled matter encounters
vast clefts, the erratic merges with cascading labyrinths. Cut,
cut, cut out the pieces, glue, glue, glue them together. Thus the
meek shall inherit the earth, but not the mineral rights, stick,
stick, stick. Snip, cut, glue, unstick and glue again! Cripple
critique! Get rid of meaning! Your mind is a nightmare that
has been eating you: now eat your mind! Cut, cut, cut... so it
seems that man is born and lives to have the substance sucked
out of him... miserable existence! Snip! Cut! Tear! Rip! Is it

so foolish to yearn for a shred of praise before death casts its posthumous judgment? Is it too much for an artist to reap a single word of encouragement before being interred in the very gloom that he alone sheds light upon! Snip! Snip! And what reward is it to be celebrated after sight has dried up and eyeballs turned to dust? Cut, cut, cut, cut, cut, cut, cut – stick! You sip on your chamomile, savour your espresso... the passage that links your mouth to your arse belches with the only truth in your body: that a hole dug six feet down awaits you as a just reward for an empty life. Cut. Between birth and death, you'll have accomplished nothing creative to have made your Mother's pain worthwhile. Snip. Your pitiful life will amount to nothing! Paste. And as a favour to Humanity, fate will gladly erase you from the memory of the World! Snip, snip, snip! Paste. Glue. Unpaste. Tear. Re-stick. Yet how he thought of death in its infinite groanings, of Aztecs ripping out living hearts and of cancer and three-year-olds buried alive and he wondered whether God was alien and cruel... he stared at the sun coming up behind the Capitol, streaking the Potomac with orange light; and then down at the outrage, the horror at his feet. Something had gone wrong between man and his creator and the evidence was here in the studio. Right here in his hand! This shape wants to be with that shape! Why? Because they are abstracted death – the very aspiration for a transcendentally reliable self-affirming beauty alloyed to those porcelain faces eaten by age – it is this abstract, fiscal, territorialised ideal that is unloved! Unloved! Cut! Stick! Glue! Rip apart! Cut again! Stick again! Paste! Glue again, start again. Everything is beautiful and nothing hurts! Snip! Ow! Bleed! Mop! Snip, snip! I put the 'fun' back in funeral! Cut! Stick! STOP!

There is a knock at the door. Something is trying to make its way in from the outside.

Chapman carefully places the safety scissors and superglue down on his cutting-out and gluing table and treads cautiously towards the door.

'Who is it?' he says, voice atremble.

'Me!'

He opens the door.

'That wasn't a particularly helpful answer.'

'Why? Who else are you expecting?'

'Not *who* but *what*...'

'I don't understand,' says Chlamydia, waving the manuscript in his face. 'If it's the story of how you got to be where you are – *where is your brother?*'

And with that the door slams shut.

Other books in this series:

Jake Chapman
The Marriage of Reason & Squalor
ISBN 978-0-9558620-0-7

Jake Chapman
Memoirs of My Writer's Block
ISBN 978-0-9563562-0-8